THE PASSPORT INVISIBLE

Published @ 2017 Trieste Publishing Pty Ltd

ISBN 9780649668069

The Passport Invisible by Perley Poore Sheehan

Edited by Trieste Publishing Pty Ltd.
Cover @ 2017

www.triestepublishing.com

PERLEY POORE SHEEHAN

THE PASSPORT INVISIBLE

 Trieste

THE
PASSPORT INVISIBLE

BY

PERLEY POORE SHEEHAN

AUTHOR OF
"THOSE WHO WALK IN DARKNESS,"
"THE BUGLER OF ALGIERS," ETC., ETC.

NEW YORK
GEORGE H. DORAN COMPANY

1916

F

77st

TO
MARY CAMPBELL MOORE
SALUTE!

CONTENTS

THE PASSPORT INVISIBLE

THE
PASSPORT INVISIBLE

CHAPTER I

OUTWARD-BOUND

AFTER a slow and clanking journey, the squalid but special and important train came to a place where the passengers were told to get down. One of these passengers was a little old lady dressed in black. A stout Swiss, with a heavy yellow moustache and a preoccupied air, lingered long enough to lend her a hand; but a guttural order from the station platform sent him nervously on his way, and the little old lady stood there unaccompanied and alone.

It was night. The sky was heavily clouded, although here and there the clouds were transiently silvered by a smothered moon. This gave to the sky an appearance oddly in harmony with that of the earth, which also was smothered in black, was also stormy, was touched up also by ephemeral and mysterious lights.

The old lady looked about her bewildered.

"Loitering forbidden," came the guttural voice. "Passengers will proceed immediately to the inspection-bureau!"

An elderly sub-officer in field-gray, his uniform offset to some measure by his spectacles and white beard, stepped out of the shadows. There was an automatic movement and click of other human shapes back there. To the old lady there came a first, groping impression that the whole place was swarming with military life. She had confidence in the military—in spite of all that she had heard. She confronted the elderly sub-officer with a smile.

"What does the high-born wish?" he demanded.

It was evident that he was the possessor of that guttural voice she had already heard. And now it was still brusque, but the tone of it was modified by a hint of wonder if not of sympathy.

"They hurried me out so fast," she replied, mildly and pleasantly, "that I couldn't get my valise down from the rack." She was speaking in a pure but rather hesitant German. "It's all the baggage I have," she added.

The elderly officer himself mounted the step of the compartment. The car was an old one. On the door was a "III," showing that it had been used in former times for third-class traffic. There were other marks about showing that this traffic might have been conducted on one of the lesser railroads in France.

There was a moment of silence. The silence was not absolute, however. It was softly jarred by a distant, perpetual grunt.

Then, off in a quarter of the sky where there had been no moonlight, the clouds were momentarily touched by a flash of weirdly green and yellow light. Followed, three muffled explosions—somewhat as if one of those grunting giants in the distance had moved up closer and relieved himself with a rumbling triple cough. A moment, and where the green and yellow light had been all was black again; the distant sounds were overcome by smaller but nearer noises.

"Is this all you had?" the sub-officer asked as he reappeared with the valise.

"Yes, and thank you so much!"

She had made a move to take the valise from his hand, but he hesitated to give it to her.

That look of wonder that had shaded his military brusqueness had now changed to amusement.

"This is no time for ladies like you to be travelling alone," he remarked.

"I've been living with a nephew in Stuttgart," she explained. "He was in the consular service. He needed me. But I was also needed—back in my own country."

"Why isn't your Herr Nephew with you now?"

Her answer came like a gentle apology: "He is dead."

The elderly sub-officer growled a barking order at the human automatons in the darkness and started along the platform without another word. The little old lady followed him.

It was a half hour later when she emerged from a dressing-room where she and such other women as had been on the train were submitted to the final search. She was in a narrow corridor, dimly lit, as bare of furniture as a jail. Along this she was ushered by the woman who had searched her. The woman threw open a door, and the little old lady entered an office in which there were half a dozen officers grouped about a table over which there was a brilliant light.

This light was so arranged as to shine strongly on the table itself and any one who might stand in front of it.

She stood there in the brilliant glare mild and unafraid. She was eighty at least. She couldn't have weighed more than a hundred pounds. She wore a black bonnet, the black silken strings of which were tied under her chin somewhat to one side. Her white but slightly yellow hair, of the tone of old ivory, descended smoothly under the bonnet over her temples. The delicately withered skin of her cheeks and throat looked as if it might have the feel and the fragrance of a white-rose petal.

"So you are leaving us?"

"Yes," she breathed.

There was a quality about her eyes and her voice whenever she spoke as if she had just recognised a friend.

As a matter of fact, it was several seconds before she could see at all the face of the man who addressed her. Eventually, she saw that he was young; that there was a disfiguring scar over half the face, but that in spite of this the face was still comely. His hands she saw readily enough. They were in the full glare of the bewildering light. One of the hands was drawn and stiff. The other was supple and fine. The owner of the hands was fingering her passport.

"This is all right," he drawled, pleasantly enough; and he pronounced the name with no trace of a German accent, "Mrs. Sylvia Nichols. But there is something else." He paused. "You know the regulations, doubtless, about the taking of unauthorised writings out of the country."

"I do, Herr General."

By this time she was able to distinguish enough of his uniform to be aware of his rank. There were many young generals in Germany.

"The enemies of the empire," he went on, without malice, "stop at nothing—not even at death." He jerked out a short laugh and glanced at his companion officers who were grouped dimly back of him. He went a trifle grim for all his amiability. "We are overrun with spies. Faster than we can shoot them they keep bobbing up." He flicked the passport aside and revealed something else he had been holding. "What is the meaning of this —Mrs. Nichols?"

In spite of the concealed menace in the question and what he had just said, Mrs. Nichols had that same smiling movement with which she might have recognised a friend.

"Ah, those—" she began, with a tremulous and soothing accent.

But the young general raised a hand as a signal for silence.

"Three envelopes!" he drawled.

He held up the flat packet of papers which he had been holding under the passport, but he kept his eyes on the gentle old traveller in front of him. The eyes were stern at first. Doubtless he intended that they remain so, but they softened.

"Three envelopes," he repeated, "and by such means the enemies of the Fatherland might cause the death of more brave men. I believe you've been merely indiscreet. See, I shall burn them."

There was a small alcohol lamp, of the kind used to melt sealing-wax, on the table to one side of him. He made a movement as if to thrust the papers into the tiny and all but invisible blue flame. But while he did so he was still watching the old lady's face.

"Oh," she murmured softly, "I wouldn't do that, Herr General!"

"Why not?"

"They're very dear to me."

"And to our enemies, perhaps!"

"No—I believe not—Herr General."

He withdrew the packet from the vicinity of the flame.

"Then I shall have to submit them to investigation. This will take time. In the meantime I shall have to detain you."

The traveller smiled at him.

"Whatever you do will be for the best, Herr General. I'm not afraid. Not for the world would I have you get into trouble on my account—"

"The gracious lady is considerate."

"You see, I had a boy like you once. I understand what your duties are. But I can assure you that you need not be afraid. Your secret agents must have already investigated me—and even those papers—weighed them—felt of them—discovered the nature of their contents."

"Which was—"

"Love!"

"Explain yourself!"

"They are letters," she said, with a sort of complacent warmth; "oh, the dearest letters in the world! One of them was written by my husband. Another was written by my son. The third—that was written by my granddaughter. They are about all that I have left of any value."

The young general studied the light packet in his hand. There was no occasion for haste. There was a certain reason for delay.

Three envelopes there were, sure enough. They were of different sizes, but they were neatly tied together by a thin silk ribbon of an old-fashioned flowered design. At least two of the envelopes, moreover, were yellow with age, and of these two one was manifestly much older than the other. The third envelope was comparatively new. Yet there was something homogeneous about the packet—somewhat as if that old-fashioned ribbon was a badge and symbol of that thing the old lady had said the envelopes contained.

"So!" drawled the officer.

"I've carried them over my heart," Mrs. Nichols explained. A faint flush of rose colour came into her cheeks and her breath quickened. She must have been very beautiful when she was young. She was very beautiful now. "But when we neared the frontier I put them into my valise to avoid any appearance of keeping them concealed."

"Two of these," said the young general, lifting the corners of the envelopes without disturbing the ribbon, "are military. How is this?—both forwarded on behalf of a Lieuten-

ant Nichols? And yet—a discrepancy—of
thirty-five years!"

"Father and son, Herr General! My husband! My boy!"

There was a quaver of love—of something
almost greater than love—in the old lady's
voice as she said this. It was love plus faith
and pride, and also of an old sorrow with no
trace of bitterness left in it. All this showed,
as well, in the subdued brilliance of her clear
eyes.

"Beautiful!" murmured the young general
reflectively.

CHAPTER II

PASSED BY THE CENSOR

PERHAPS you have heard about the battle of Chickamauga," said Mrs. Nichols with tender enthusiasm. "My husband was there. We hadn't been married very long. I was very proud of him."

"I've studied the battle of Chickamauga."

"Of course the number of troops engaged was not so great as in the battles of to-day," Mrs. Nichols went on, "but they were all men of the same stock—with the same sort of courage—and the same sort of devotion. I've talked to many of them who were fighting then —both North and South. That's why it means so much to me to be—American!"

One would have said that something of Mrs. Nichols' age left her as she made this statement. That slight flush that had come into her delicate cheeks had remained. Her voice, for all its soft mildness, was faintly proud and vibrant.

"The country down around Chickamauga Creek," she explained, "was rough and wooded. There were hardly any good maps. So it came about that a single company on one side might be confronting a regiment on the other—hand to hand—through the woods—"

"*Ja-wohl!*"

"That first letter was sent to me by a Southern gentleman—himself a lieutenant, but for the South. He knew that otherwise the letter might never reach me, nor any one tell me how brave that last stand had been—"

"Why?"

"Because my husband's comrades had all been killed. But you may imagine how proud I was, after the peace was signed, when that Southern gentleman came all the way from his home in Alabama, although wounded himself, to tell me how David's dying thought had been of me, and that our firstborn—you see I'd written to him about it—should be—a boy."

"And was it?"

"Yes."

"And he—"

"Is that other Lieutenant Nichols whose letter is there—also written to me—also incomplete—also, therefore, you might say, a link

between this world and the next. He went to
Cuba with Colonel Roosevelt.''

"Ha! A Rough Rider!"

There was a slight murmur. Mrs. Nichols
proceeded: "He was so like his father! He
couldn't resist the call. I—I was glad to see
him go—and to know that the country was
united again; for in the same troop with David
Jr., was the son of that Southern gentleman who
had fought on the other side in our Civil War.
Langley was his name—Jesse Langley; and
David loved him.''

There was a momentary lull. There was a
subdued movement at one of the doors. But
the young general with the scar on his face
listened to what the old lady said with the air
of one who is rapt in thought. So did the
others.

"I tried not to regret," whispered Mrs.
Nichols, "even when I learned that he lay out
there in the burning sun, with the land-crabs
rattling about, for almost a day and a night
and another day before he died. For he died
as his father had died before him, under the
same flag, also a lieutenant, in an army of—
liberation!''

The young general bestirred himself.

"What is this third letter?"

"From my son's daughter. Perhaps—I pray not, but—perhaps the last letter I may receive from her. She also is in the shadow—"

"A woman!"

"As your own mother would understand, Herr General. I hope you still have her with you. She must be proud of you."

"I see," said the general with a touch of gallantry. "The daughter of your soldier-son is herself—"

"About to become a mother."

For almost a minute, possibly, the young general continued to reflect. He scowled slightly, but that was merely a reflex of his training; there was no anger in his mood.

Three or four times he made a move with those pitifully unmated hands of his to take the ribbon from the envelopes, open them, make them disgorge whatever else they might hold concealed. He listened to the hoarse whispers of those about him. But he did not turn his head. Most of the time his eyes kept coming back to the face of Mrs. Sylvia Nichols—kept coming back as if in spite of himself.

When he spoke, his words were an abrupt growl but there was no unkindliness in them.

"A little packet of old love-letters!" he said. He looked at Mrs. Nichols with final decision.

"Have I your word—as a soldier's widow—and as the mother of a soldier—that you are concealing nothing?"

"You have, Herr General!"

"I am asking you this chiefly for your own protection," he went on, dropping back into his clipped professional drawl. "You have been long enough in Germany, and on this earth, to know that military necessity is a harsh master. Our enemies, as I do not have to remind you again, are numerous and cunning."

He passed the letters over to her, but he still held them a moment even when her own hand was upon them.

"I do not exaggerate," he said. It was the man, and not the soldier, who was speaking now. "There is a deadly danger to any one found with unauthorised papers in his possession. At this very moment,"—he gave a quick glance about him—"certain papers of the Empire are in hostile hands. It will go hard with whosoever is discovered with these papers in his—or her—possession. Even you, my gracious lady!—neither your age nor your—your holiness!—would save you."

Mrs. Nichols' only response was a look of appreciation.

"Out there," the general continued, rising

to his feet, "is the Lake of Constance. We're going to put you on a boat. In two hours—God willing!—you and the others will be in Switzerland. But the arm of the Empire is long. It reaches—and strikes!—around the world."

Mrs. Nichols, with the return of that same faint flush which had already warmed her soft cheeks, soberly returned the packet of letters to their familiar hiding-place in her breast.

For a moment longer her eyes glowed softly back at the officer's own.

"Thank you, Herr General," she said gently. "You are young. You are generous. I hope that—when all this is over—your mother will have the joy of welcoming you home again."

The general permitted himself the suspicion of a smile. But he checked any other sentiment he might have felt. He barked a military order from his throat, and at that a soldier clumped out from somewhere in the darkness. The soldier carried the black valise. Nonetheless he halted rigidly, snapped a machinelike salute.

"This man will show you to the boat," said the young general. "I have the honour to wish you"—he himself touched the spiked helmet he wore—"good-by and good luck!"

CHAPTER III

TOKEN FOR TOKEN

THE night appeared to be blacker than ever. The clouds had won at least a temporary victory over the moon. Aloft no ray of light was visible whatsoever, and below it was only a little better. There, Mrs. Nichols could sense the wide railroad yard about her—in the dancing arcs of a few goblin lanterns, the occasional flare from a fire-box, the mumbled puffing of exhausts and the clank of iron.

But the engines which were sputtering and drilling about were without headlights and, for the most part, as black as night-prowling monsters. The inspection building itself was black. And it was through a black shed and out onto a black wharf that the soldier led the traveller to where a black steamer lay.

Even the Lake of Constance was dark—as dark as the sky; the dim constellations which swarm its shores in ordinary times were likewise invisible.

"What is this place, my son?" Mrs. Nichols inquired.

"Manzell, perhaps, high-born," he answered humbly; "or maybe yet it's Friedrichshafen."

She didn't press him. The guess was good enough. The general himself had said that within a couple of hours or so she would be in Switzerland. That was the important thing. And trains that carried civilians—especially foreign civilians and potential enemies—were perpetually being shunted about into strange corners and over strange routes.

Four sentinels guarded the dimly lighted gangplank of the steamer. An officer with a face that glowered sullenly out of the darkness appeared in front of Mrs. Nichols and her soldier-guide the moment they stepped on deck. The soldier halted rigidly and snapped his machinelike salute. In response to an order, the soldier then dropped the valise to the deck, wheeled, and disappeared the way he had come. Mrs. Nichols picked up her valise. She made her way around to the other side of the boat—there where lay in front of her nothing but the dark waters of the tranquil lake, and, beyond these, the invisible shores of Switzerland.

It brought a quickening touch of emotion to

her heart merely to think of it—Switzerland!
—a long step toward home.

Her eyes became accustomed to the darkness,
until the darkness itself seemed to become a
sort of blue radiance that emanated from the
lake and held the whole world about her in
solution. It was magical, and healing, and
holy—as she saw it; a possible reflex, she ad-
mitted, of her own state of mind.

The death of her nephew in Stuttgart hadn't
affected her so much. The planet itself was as
if mortally wounded and bleeding to death.
But it was the hope that affected her—the hope
one of those three letters contained. To her
only grandchild—the only daughter of him who
had been her only son—a child, please God,
was now to be born! A boy, O Lord! A boy
who would be as his father had been, and his
father's father!

She drew the packet of letters from her
breast. She held them to her lips. There in
the mystic solvent of the night, which made
the material and spiritual worlds as one, and
also the past and the present, her own spirit
darted and soared, ringed and stooped, like an
etherial falcon in brightest sunshine.

She was a girl again—in crinoline, just married, with the magic and mystery of love still

fresh upon her, and upon *him*, and the world;
she heard the heart-thrilling music of the fifes
and drums, saw the long, long columns in light
blue. Many of those boys she had known then
wore their hair rather long and were as beautiful as girls; but none of them was so beautiful as David, sashed and gauntleted, booted and
spurred, on his black horse, that look of sober
tenderness in his eyes.

She knew as well as if she had been there
that that was his look the day he lay dying in
the woods along the Chickamauga.

"David!" she whispered.

But the name was an evocation of that other
David—their boy, reared in his father's tradition.

Things had changed in '98. The uniforms
were different. So was the music. And the
soldiers—they had seemed younger even, for
the most part, than had the boys of '61. The
spirit, though, was the same. That never
changed. Only, this time, the second David
had sought out the son of that Southern veteran who had seen the first David die, and
Northerner and Southerner had found means
to enter the same regiment.

Jesse Langley, of Alabama, and David Nichols, of Vermont! Troopers under the same

flag! And away—away to San Antonio, where the East and the West, the North and the South, Pawnees and cowboys, yachtsmen and rangers, college-boys and desperadoes, gamblers and frontier-preachers, were assembling in a single brotherhood for the greatest of all adventures—the bartering of life against the chance to serve America!

Why, Jesse Langley's father who, only yesterday—so it seemed—was the dashing Lieutenant Langley, C. S. A., had wanted to go. Jo Wheeler was going; wasn't he?

But the old Southerner, like so many warriors of the Lost Cause, could only send his son —and his allegiance—to the Stars and Stripes —and his gallant compliments to those who lived in what had once been hostile territory. So Mrs. Nichols and Lieutenant Langley, C. S. A., had thus exchanged their last pledge of union.

For the veteran was dead by the time the battle of San Juan Hill was fought, and his son— the second Jesse Langley—was promoted for gallantry and himself became a lieutenant. Then, as his father had done before him, this Jesse Langley had gone North to tell Sylvia Nichols how her second Lieutenant Nichols, this time her son, had died in the service.

"Carrying a message from Woods to Roosevelt—and he delivered it, too!"

She remembered how young Langley, just as his father had done, had smiled at her with tears in his eyes as he told her; how there was the same note of pride in his voice; and the same flush of pride in her own heart. She would not have had it otherwise.

And now the second David's child, her grandchild, had grown up to beautiful young womanhood, was married. Once more the country was girding up its strength and purifying its heart for the sacrificial rite of justice and liberty among men.

In the blue night, Mrs. Nichols saw this last child of her heart, she who, even now, might also be facing death—as all women must, that the life of the world go on.

She was standing there like that, as absorbed in her reflections as if she had been in church and the world at peace, when she heard a quick, light step. A moment later some one had addressed her, in English, with an accent that was familiar.

"Are you an American?"

"Yes!"

She was wondering why the stranger, whoever he was—himself an American, as she in-

stantly guessed—should have spoken so softly
and breathlessly; what it could have mattered
to him what her nationality might be. But she
had responded with that quick and gentle smile
of hers.

"I thought so," he answered. "Thank God
I was right!"

He paused to look about him. He seemed
to be reassured by the empty stretch of unlighted deck. He turned to her again in the
blue obscurity. She saw that he was young—
not more than twenty-five or twenty-six; and
handsome, in a dashing, gallant way. There
was something about him to recall her own boy
—he who had died.

It was as if the two of them were friendly
ghosts.

Perhaps something of this came into the
young man's thought as well. He peered into
her face.

"I'm going to trust you," he thrilled. "I
learned—no matter how—that there was an
American lady, homeward-bound, on this boat.
The moment that I saw you I knew that you
must be she. But I had to ask. I had to be
sure."

He was speaking rapidly, with a suppressed
enthusiasm that was somehow joyful. Mrs.

Nichols remarked the voice. There was a singing quality in it even now when it was little more than a whisper.

"Can I be of any service?" she asked, with gentle interest.

"Yes," he answered. "Stand here beside me at the rail—where there will be less danger from eavesdroppers—and also where I can keep an eye out in case they come."

"Who are 'they'?"

"My pursuers!"

Mrs. Nichols looked up into his face. There glinted into her mind the things that the young general back there had told her concerning spies and certain papers.

"Boy," she breathed.

"Yes!"

"I understand. Don't be afraid."

"Oh," he almost sobbed with suppressed emotion which no one could have classified, whether joy or grief; "there was only one thing that I feared—and that—that was not death!"

CHAPTER IV

UNDER ORDERS

STEADY," breathed Mrs. Nichols.

She could see that the youth was in a state of nervous tension. She could see that there was a physical as well as a mental and spiritual cause for this. He had been well dressed, but he was travel-worn. His face was drawn with fatigue. The fire in his eyes was feverish.

"I have certain papers," he said.

"I've heard about them."

"But not all."

"No."

"They have to be delivered—"

"Where?"

"Washington!"

"I'll help you. Just tell me how."

The youth hesitated. His eyes had scarcely left her, but he was in a quiver of watchfulness. Suddenly he seized one of her hands in both of his and pressed it to his lips.

"I can't go any further," he exclaimed.

"Why not?"

"I'm trapped."

"Is there no way—"

"No way out," he replied. "There were two others. They've been killed. Now Gracken and his men—Gracken's the chief of the Intelligence Department—"

He stopped and acutely listened.

"God knows your need," whispered Mrs. Nichols.

"When you speak like that, it's as if you were my mother. And when I first saw you—"

"Just act as if I were your mother."

There was a wavering moment.

"Oh, may I?" he cried softly. "I've been alone—alone!"

Impulsively his arms went about her. She was small and slender but it was as if he had found a tower of strength. He stood there for a moment, head bowed, recovering his peace and strength.

"There's Gracken himself," he said. "You'll know him by his broad shoulders and his wooden leg, and a whole army of spies— one especially—a girl, Ruth Bancroft, who pretends to be an American—" He interrupted himself: "Oh, I can't let you take the risk!"

"You must—if it's the only way."

"You were sent," he whispered, "by God Himself!"

It must have been a spectacle for the angels —these two who had never seen each other before, who even now did not know each other's name, standing there as if they actually were mother and son. But no one else saw. The narrow deck still remained mercifully deserted. The night was a curtain about them.

"I'll take the papers," Mrs. Nichols said.

"Straight to Washington!"

"And then?"

"Into the hands of the President! No one else must see them or suspect! Oh, if you only could!"

"I can."

"But the danger!"

"Not a sparrow shall fall—without our Father—"

"But if they discover you have them—"

"I'll ask His help!"

Mrs. Nichols, calm with the serenity of her age and sex, was looking up into the boy's face. Her heart yearned for him—he was so young, so gallant, so harried, so brought to bay. She could feel the slight tremor of the arms that held her close to him. But this was a mere reaction. She could see by his expression that his mind was at work, and that he felt no fear.

"I believe you'll do it," he said. "But I can't let you undertake it without your understanding fully all that it means."

"I do understand."

"No pains under heaven will be spared to intercept these papers—prevent the President from getting them. You'll have against you all the might—and cruelty—"

"Son, there is a greater Might!"

"Little mother!"

"Her you can trust."

"I believe you," he whispered soberly. "Listen; I don't know how much time remains to us, but there won't be much. In a minute or so they'll know that I'm on the boat, and then—"

"Give me the papers."

"Even if it does put your life in danger?"

"Yes."

"See—mother!—I'll pass them to you. Put them out of sight. Careful, now! We may be watched, even now."

"Are there any other instructions?"

"Only those I've mentioned. They're more precious than life—as precious as our honour. Straight to Washington; then—*into the hands of the President!*"

All the time that he had been saying this he had continued to hold Mrs. Nichols in his arms. His feverish eyes seemed supernaturally large. She could see there was something else he wanted to say, but she waited in silence.

He put his hand into the breast-pocket of his coat. She was following instructions. Any one who might be watching would never suspect what was taking place. Into her fingers she felt the thrust of a number of crinkling sheets of thin oiled paper. She coughed slightly, putting her hand to her breast. When the fit of coughing had passed, the papers had disappeared.

"Three sheets," the boy whispered.

"They're safe."

In the momentary silence that followed there again came that subdued, huge, barely perceptible and yet thrilling grunt from the distance. Big guns!—possibly thirty miles away!—the irregular pulse of a delirious world!

They both felt it. Into the minds of each of them must have come the thought that so, sometime, no one could tell how soon, would come the pulse of America.

"There was something else," whispered Mrs. Nichols.

"Yes! If anything happens to me—her

name is Thomas. She lives in Wooster, Ohio. Tell her I couldn't write—"

"Your mother?"

"Yes! I'm Samuel P. Thomas."

"I'll not forget!"

"She looks like you."

He paused, while that unearthly quality put into his face by the darkness—and impending events, perhaps—became intensified.

"And I," she responded softly, "had a boy —who looked like you."

"What became of him?"

"He died—for his country—as his father did."

"Now," the boy exclaimed, "I do know!"

What the knowledge was he did not say, but the quality of it shone in his face, subtly translated itself into some hint of final relief and confidence that had not been his before.

"And you are glad?" she whispered.

"Glad!"

"So will your mother be. I know!"

"Grant me a final boon—that I may kiss you and her—good-by!"

She smiled up at him, whitely, in the darkness.

The real romances of this life are doubtless often made up of the most unpromising elements. This is but another way of saying, perhaps, that to the supreme Imaginer there are no unpromising elements—not of the human kind.

As Samuel P. Thomas, of Wooster, Ohio, brought his lips reverently to the soft cheek of this old lady who had appeared as if indeed Godsent in his hour of need, he had a reeling sense of romance such as he had never known before. So must his own soul have felt—some voice was telling him—when that soul first encountered his mother's and received the promise of incarnation.

Perhaps this was the universal mother whose cheek he kissed!

Her faint perfume penetrated to the very spirit of him—an atmosphere of geraniums and lavender, as the perfume of his own mother had reached him, on Sunday mornings, when he was a little boy, in church, and him sleeping the sermon away with his head under her tender arm.

Sylvia Nichols also had closed her eyes.

Into her thought as well the circumstances were such as to bring a baffling and heavenly confusion.

More than half a century ago a strong young man who was going out to die had thus held her in his arms. That was her husband. Almost a score of years ago another strong young man, prepared to make the same sacrifice, had done the same. That was her son. Now, here was the same cosmic drama about to be repeated.

The cadence of the barely heard cannon across the night became as the beating of drums. Deftly and so faintly as to be inaudible to physical hearing came the fine shrill of fifes —*"The girl I left behind me!"*—and the low, muffled thunder of a regiment that marched— the rolling, louder thunder of a regiment that sang, and crowds that cheered—louder and louder, to the flashing of flags, and horses, and steel, until it was like the very voice of the Lord of Hosts!

And all the time her heart was whispering to her that as those other two had died, so this boy must die.

She opened her eyes and smiled again.

So did Thomas.

CHAPTER V

FAREWELL!

UP the guarded gangplank of the black little steamer there had come a group of men. One of these was a man in civilian dress with hugely wide shoulders and the lopsided but efficient gait which so often goes with the possession of a wooden leg. Gracken, no doubt, from the description that had been given of him by the young American. Accompanying Gracken were five soldiers commanded by a sergeant. There were three other civilians, yet these also were of a military appearance, though shifty and quick.

Arrived at the head of the gangplank the group paused. The squad of soldiers was left there to supplement the sentinels already on duty, while Gracken—he who commanded the party—issued whispered orders to his civilian friends. And these thereupon scattered.

It was only a few moments later that Samuel P. Thomas and Mrs. Sylvia Nichols became aware that they no longer had the dark deck to themselves. They had withdrawn from the rail of the boat and now stood in the heavy shadow of a ventilator. Still, each could see the other's face clearly enough—each an American, bound together by the vision of the Union.

"And now," whispered Mrs. Nichols, "your mind may be easy."

"It is. I'll play my last trick on them. I'll throw them off the trail."

"How?"

"Watch! I hear them coming!"

"Good-by! God bless you, son!"

Samuel P. Thomas had again seized her hand. He pressed it against his cheek, touched it again to his lips.

"And the Lord be with you," he whispered hastily. His voice was almost joyful. "Into the hands of the President! Now I go. Good-by—little mother!"

He flashed a final look into her eyes. He turned and walked rapidly away. It was just as Gracken, with his broad shoulders and stomping timber-foot rounded an angle of the deck-house.

Gracken was not alone. Nor were his actions unco-ordinated with those of his associates who had come on board with him. Two shadowy forms suddenly appeared not far behind him. Two other shadowy forms appeared down the deck in the direction young Thomas had taken. Mrs. Nichols, leaning against the rail of the boat, became a witness to this and all that followed, she herself as unnoticed as if she had been but one more shadow in those hurrying shadows of the vaster night.

In her heart though, as she waited and watched, her supplication was flaming like a torch.

Briskly the young American agent stepped away along the dark deck. He must have known that a fight was at hand. More likely than not he had even recognised those two shadowy shapes who suddenly sought to intercept him. But he was too old a tactician to give any warning of what he expected to do.

As his enemies closed in upon him, themselves acting with apparent carelessness, the American agent gave a slanting spring. There followed a sprawling tussle. There were a few moments of straining confusion. Out of this the American emerged. Followed a rippling flash of fire, perhaps a dozen crowded shots.

Gracken and his men joined the chase.

Little Mrs. Nichols, standing there at the railing like a mere frail wraith of womanhood, knew that thus far at least her prayers had been answered. For she had seen the youth who had kissed her good-by disappear into the darkness of the after-deck, and he had not run like a wounded man.

There were other indications immediately following that he still had his enemies worried.

Hitherto the night had been as if held in the grip of a huge suppression. Suddenly this grip had begun to relax. There was a flare of light, blinding and swift, where no light had been. Out of the coagulated darkness immense forms, ungainly and colossal, revealed themselves as they might have done at the first word of Creation. The same fiat broke the void of sound, for the first pistol-shots had been followed by others—then the heavier detonations of high-power rifles.

In an interval of time which might have been measurable in seconds, or even in minutes, but which seemed instantaneous, the whole port had become a medley of jagged contrast—massed lights and massed darknesses, shaking sounds and almost equally shaking silences.

Three or four searchlights had begun to play about. When the firing ceased there was a chorus of muffled speech.

Then there was a concentrated din of both speech and shots.

Back of where the steamer lay, Mrs. Nichols was now able to discern the bulky outlines of a dozen great barges. Then along the bulwark of one of these she saw the figure of a man appear just as a searchlight picked him up. He was dwarfed by his surroundings. He was hatless and otherwise unkempt. But Mrs. Nichols recognised him. It was her American.

Instantly there came a fresh crash of rifle-fire. But so far he seemed to have miraculously escaped.

He sought now to get out of range of the searchlight, but that long accusing finger of illumination stuck to him cruelly. He leaped for the blackness and momentarily disappeared. Then a searchlight from another quarter picked him up. He was smiling. He was fighting a losing fight, but there was no mistake about that smile. The searchlight brought out every line of his unshielded face, revealed every emotion of it.

He was still smiling, a moment later, when he slumped a little to one side in response to another volley, and clapped a hand to his left arm. Struck!

But he wasn't done for. Not yet!

More cautiously, in spite of the fusillade that had him for a target, and disregarding now the concentrated glare of all the searchlights that were on him, he made his way along the edge of the next scow and looked out in the direction of the last barge of all.

Between it and the hulk where he stood there was a gap of open water possibly six or seven feet wide.

He studied this distance. He looked back of him. There was no more firing. But it wasn't a respite they were granting him. Out from the shore, from barge to barge, and scattering as they advanced, came at least a score of pursuers. There was shouting, then silence. The American had jumped.

He had fallen a little short, but he was clinging to the side of the barge—one of his arms wounded, but still capable of some use, evidently.

Slowly, he dragged himself up. He sat there for a moment resting. He shook his head. He lifted his face. He was still smiling.

Once more the shots crashed.

But this time they seemed to electrify him. He was on his feet. He gave one look at his pursuers. Then he was running to the outermost rim of the barge—while those searchlights clung to him like ghostly hounds. There was a louder shout than ever when his pursuers discovered his intention. One of the foremost of these pursuers was Gracken, with his huge shoulders and wooden leg.

Gracken himself threw down a hand he had been holding aloft and from the hand there spat the rippling crash of an automatic pistol.

But Gracken had fired too late.

The American had thrown his own hands above his head and dived into the sheltering waters of the lake.

CHAPTER VI

HIS UTMOST ALL

CLEAR and vivid—for at least that one among the spectators—was the unfolding vision of all that followed. Mrs. Nichols still stood where the boy had left her. As so many human beings before her—and mothers especially perhaps—she saw that those prayers of hers were by way of fulfillment although not in the way she had designed or expected.

First of all, out there on the black and silver surface of the lake were the widening ripples where the American had disappeared. For a breathless period that was all—just those drifting circles in the white downpour of the searchlights.

Was he never to rise again?

As if the superhuman searchlights themselves were in an anguish of doubt these began to fidget, then waver, then shift about. Back again they came—to hold steady—to seize again upon some fresh circle of secretive depth.

50

Then a something appeared. His head!
Even in that tense and unearthly moment of
suspense there was time enough for a mother
to divine just what a man's head meant in the
romance of the earth. It was a temple. It
was a shrine. It was a treasure-house of
knowledge—of memories gay and sombre—
memories of a little town named Wooster, and
of the great capitol at Washington, and of the
Statue of Liberty in the Harbour of New York.
The head came up, and they were shooting at
it again. All around it rose the little leaning
geysers of water where the bullets struck.

The searchlights fastened on the spectacle
with a sort of white, unholy greed—as if they
couldn't see enough.

Then once more the surface of the water was
deserted.

The interval was not so long before the next
appearance of the fugitive. Not more than ten
feet or so had he been able to swim under water.
But that ten feet—or whatever the distance
was—had been in the direction of the place
where Sylvia Nichols stood.

And this time his face was toward her. She
was even sure that she had seen him smile for
the last time. He was a great actor in that
deadly spotlight—with the lake for his stage,

with earth and heaven as parquet and gallery.

For this is what he did:

Up went the one good arm that remained to him. In the upstretched hand there was something white—whether handkerchief or papers, who could tell? He waved his hand.

"To me, O God!"

It was a cry straight from the heart of the little old lady in black—the maternal vicar, the mother by proxy, the one other representative of his land and race there to behold. As a sacred duty she held steadfast while the bullets resumed their diabolic tattoo.

She closed her eyes for a moment only when a cheer went up, and she knew that he had died.

Out of this clarity of vision as to material things, there came a perception no less clear as to the meaning back of it all.

There could no longer be any doubt—even if doubt had been possible before—as to the profound and cogent significance of everything that the boy had told her.

Those papers which she now had in her possession were of vital importance to her country and to her country's enemies. Into the hands of the President of the United States and of none other were those papers now to be delivered.

Once before had she been in Washington. That also had been in wartime.

Eyes closed, but as one gazing at something very far away, she stood there with her face up-lifted. She could see it again—the dome of the Capitol. She could feel it again—that surge of devotion in her heart such as had been there that other time. It was a day in June, and the atmosphere was a blaze of blue and gold. There was a light breeze from across the Poto-mac—tepid and fragrant, wholesome and pure —the breath of Columbia herself!—and in this the flag fluttered and waved—upward!—as if to friends on high.

She remembered with what trepidation and yet with what faith she had gone up the steps of the White House, how she had waited with many other people—women, officers in uniform, grave and important civilians—until a young secretary, deft and gentle, had summoned her into an inner room.

And there she was in the presence of the great man she had come to see.

"Mr. Lincoln!"

She had intended to call him Mr. President, but he had pretended not to notice her mistake.

All he did was to take her by the hand and

thank her for what David Nichols had done that
day on the banks of the Chickamauga. Just a
few simple and homely words, doubtless; but
why had she gone away with such fierce and
flaming gladness in her heart?

"Oh, Mr. Lincoln!" she whispered now.

And her mind translated his image, solemn
and sweet, into the semblance of his successor
—he who was in the White House now, the
scholar who no less walked alone, he who was
weighted with a burden no less colossal, he who
also prophesied with a voice that reached all
the peoples of the earth.

So intense had been her thought that she had
failed to rotice it when the steamer left its
berth and began its trembling, lurching trip
across the lake. But presently, when she
opened her eyes, the blue grotto of the lake had
become infinite. Then, precisely as if all this
darkness had been artificial—and was no longer
necessary, the first act of the drama having been
played—the clouds rifted majestically to let
down an indescribable flood of moonlight.

It was a light to give as none other a haunted
quality to this already haunted night. It was
as if the universe, and all the creatures of it,
and even the Creator Himself, were assembled

here in this place which had become a Judgment Hall.

"And thus am I come up before You for judgment, O Lord," said Mrs. Nichols.

Through her mind there passed a recollection of how, when a Certain Other was beset by enemies, He had passed through the midst of them unseen. Her heart was telling her that only by such intervention could she accomplish the mission which had been entrusted to her. By faith! It never occurred to her to think that she might be less favoured.

Her faith was perfect.

Nor was this faith of hers wholly a matter of old training. At least a part of it was derived from what she had just seen—the last event in the life of Samuel P. Thomas, of Wooster, Ohio.

The boy had given his utmost all that she might succeed. Were there none other, he would be standing up there now by the Judgment Seat to plead her cause.

"Would the gracious lady like a state-room where she may rest a bit?"

Mrs. Nichols turned and found a stewardess at her side.

"Thank you; I should like to lie down a little while."

The stewardess picked up the black valise from the deck and led her through a narrow companionway, then down a flight of brass-bound steps and threw open the door of a tiny cabin.

CHAPTER VII

VOTIVE OFFERINGS

MRS. NICHOLS entered this place and locked the door behind her. It was a mere cubbyhole of a state-room. On one side of it there was a berth. Opposite the door was a small washstand with a mirror and an electric light above it. In the wall opposite the berth there was a small, round port open to the night. But from the moment that Mrs. Nichols found herself alone in these cramped quarters she knew that they also were to have a place in the adventure.

She turned out the light.

There for an interval the darkness seemed absolute, but gradually once more her eyes became accustomed to the obscurity. Then, as the steamer shifted a few points on its course, the moonlight was flooding the little room as it was flooding the world outside.

But Mrs. Nichols needed no light.

Those papers of such importance which

young Thomas had entrusted to her keeping
she had thrust into the bosom of her dress
where she already had those three priceless letters which the general back there had allowed
her to keep. She took them all out and contemplated them—with a flutter at her heart.

She was very tired. She seated herself on
the edge of the berth.

It would never do to carry the papers loose.
They would have to be preserved with care.
Into the hands of the President of the United
States would she place them at last.

The papers were three in number—large
sheets of oiled or waxed paper, each sheet
folded separately and tightly. But in spite of
the fact that the sheets were so tightly folded,
and that the paper composing them was not
very thick, still the three of them made a con-
siderable bulk.

After due thought, Mrs. Nichols carefully
unknotted the ribbon which bound her own letters together and slipped one of the papers into
that envelope which contained the last communication from her granddaughter. Having
done this, she weighed the envelope in her hand,
felt of it, laid it aside.

She put one of the remaining sheets into the

envelope which bore the date of 1863, and yet the third into that envelope dated 1898.

Then she assembled the three envelopes and began to tie them together again. But even while she was doing this she was afflicted by a doubt, some whisper of conscience, that made her pause, take counsel again of the moonlit night.

Was she doing right?

She brooded, submissive and patient. She shook her head. It wasn't so much that some future examination of her packet of letters might reveal the increased bulk and weight. No, it wasn't that. She had a feeling that she would have to make her choice between them— woman's eternal choice between two loves.

The personal letters she had been permitted to keep. Why? Because they were love-letters—a packet of love-letters!

But what love of hers was greater than her love for America! None! These papers which she was to deliver into the hands of the President—were they not themselves love-letters so far as she was concerned? If she replaced the other letters by these newer and more important ones, would not her conscience then be clear?

So she reasoned.

There was something else. She believed in sacrifice. Surely, God would be on her side if He saw what a sacrifice she was ready to make now to the cause. Anyway, it was fitting that she should give up her dearest earthly possessions at a time when the fine young men of the world were giving up their lives.

Oh, happy thought!

Mrs. Nichols sighed, but straightway the sigh was followed by a look of cheerful and consecrated obedience. Any one watching her would have said she heard a voice.

Once more she spread out her precious envelopes on her lap.

This time, the first envelope she selected was the oldest one. From it she drew out that letter which was the last bit of handwriting that had ever come to her from her husband. Not a line nor a dot of it was missing from her mental sight as she contemplated it in the moonlight. The paper on which it was written was rather pulpy and thick and still in good condition, but the ink was faded. The handwriting was bold, yet elegant and aristocratic, just as the writer himself had been.

By memory she read:

Headquarters, Army of the Cumberland,
South of Chattanooga, Sept. 18, 1863.

Dearest Sylvia: You can't imagine what joy filled my heart when I received your letter about expected arrival. I imparted glad tidings to Genl. Rosecrans, and he offered me furlough, but there may be some more fighting ere long here on Chickamauga Creek, and not until it's over, little bride, can I join you and —oh, wonderful words—our firstborn—

What else was written on the yellow paper was in the handwriting of him who had then been a stranger and an enemy:

Forwarded as token of respect to gallant foe, mortally wounded.

Jesse Langley, Lieut.
C. S. A.

It brought the past very near to her, and the rocks and woods, the streams and meadows of the Tennessee country which she had visited after the war—Chattanooga, Missionary Ridge, Lookout Mountain. How the old names came back to her—Rosecrans and Bragg, Thomas and Polk, Sheridan and Longstreet, Grant and Lee! Days heroic and terrible which even now made her old heart quicken!

She pressed the letter to her lips. Then she tore the paper into tiny fragments and let it drift from the open porthole into the churned waters of the lake.

This much accomplished she felt more certain than ever that what she had decided to do was right. There was that same sadness in her breast as she took the letter from the second envelope and contemplated it as she had the first. It was the letter from her son. He had started to write it immediately after the arrival of his regiment at Daiquiri, in Cuba.

Such enthusiasm! He and his partner, Langley, had not been left behind! They had already shelled the Spaniards, so what did it matter if they had hardly anything to eat, or drink, or wear!—or that the land-crabs and vultures, the jungle and the steaming soil were all unfriendly!—or that there was no transport except what a fellow could carry on his back!

There was a reference to the wonderful feeling that came to him when he first went under fire at Las Guasimas:

When the bullets began to whine through the jungle, I knew what it was to live! I wasn't frightened. I can't be. Here as I write in my little old tent I feel your spirit hovering over me as if I were still in the cradle with you on watch. I'll write soon again.

But he never did.

She could follow him now, as she followed him then—up through the Cuban jungle by that narrow path which led from Las Guasimas on toward the San Juan hills.

To Santiago also she had gone, when the war was over, to find the place—with young Lieutenant Langley to guide her—where her boy lay buried. Jungle and palms, tropical heat and a strange dark people; but these also had become the familiar elements of her spiritual life; just as had the names of Wheeler, and Wood, and Roosevelt, of Tampa, El Caney, and Montauk Point!

"Son!" she murmured. "This is what you and your father would have me do."

For, with no hesitation now, she began to tear up the second letter. And, all the time that she was doing this, the feeling grew stronger and stronger that only in this way could she make sure of the mission that had been entrusted to her. It was a feeling that not only would she be successful but that she was successful already.

She drew out the last letter of all.

"You're of the old stock too, Marjorie," she whispered. "God be with you, and all young mothers!"

But she was suffering from a certain reaction by the time that the last of those sacrosanct fragments had drifted out into the night. She tottered a little as she turned from the porthole. She felt very much in need of rest. It would be a good thing to lie down for a while.

So she untied her bonnet-ribbons, and removing the bonnet, hung it up. But even greater than her need of rest was a greater need which now overwhelmed her.

At the side of the berth she knelt and bowed her head on her folded hands.

CHAPTER VIII

THE LONG ARM

COUNT OTTO VON GRACKEN, chief of that section of the Imperial spy service—otherwise Intelligence Department—thus far baffled by Samuel P. Thomas, late of Wooster, Ohio, and Washington, D. C., turned slowly in his chair to confront the man he had summoned.

"What result?" he rasped.

"Nothing, Excellency."

Gracken muttered a curse, but he was not the man to lose his energy in futile wrath. If anything, his broad and smoothly shaven face merely displayed the expression of a yet more concentrated and cunning thought.

"Sit down, Max," he said pleasantly enough after a moment.

Max was a tall young man, lean and graceful. Apart from a certain cruel and shifty quality of his gray eyes he was good to look

at. He dropped into a chair and awaited his
superior's pleasure.

They were in a small office on the second
floor of that building through which Mrs. Sylvia Nichols had passed the night before in the
course of her final investigation before leaving
Germany.

"Autopsy reveal anything?" Gracken asked.

"It revealed the truth of your surmise," Max
responded, "that our American did not swal-
low those papers of his. We are proceeding
with our search of the lake."

"It will do no harm," was Gracken's com-
ment; "nor good! Those papers were too val-
uable for Thomas to have thrown them away—
especially if there was any chance of our getting them. No, he hung on to them even after
he knew that he didn't have one chance in a
million to get away with his life; and he did this
when he knew that he might have saved his life
by turning them back to us. For that matter,
had he merely been content to destroy them he
could have touched a match to them as readily
as he could light a cigarette."

"What then?"

"The papers are still in existence."

"And Thomas still had them an hour before
his death."

"That means that in that last hour he either mailed them or handed them over to a confederate."

"He has been the only suspect in this part of the Empire."

"If he succeeded in blinding us so long," said Gracken, "there are others capable of doing as much and more. I might as well tell you now, Max, that I have my suspicions."

"Of whom?"

"The young lady known as Number Three-Thirty-Nine."

Max did not answer for a moment. A few fine beads of perspiration came out on his brow—a phenomenon which did not escape the keen eyes of his superior.

"You mean—Miss Bancroft?"

"Ah, my words strike home, do they?" Gracken taunted, genially.

"That young lady is nothing to me," said Max, forcing his shifty eyes to meet the steady gaze of the other. "What makes you suspect her, if I may ask?"

"The answer is simple," Gracken replied. "I've used her more than once to get secrets from young men employed by our enemies. She has never failed before. You may reply that she was not going to fail this time—that she would have succeeded in getting the papers from Thomas had she had more time.''

''Where is she now?''

''Waiting—waiting for him over in Aborn—but whether in the expectancy of business or pleasure I cannot tell. I am of the opinion, though, that it will be something of a shock to her when she learns of the events of last night. I have sent a wireless—by the usual route; but it was not to her. I am having her watched. If I have reason to believe that she deceived me—''

There was a sinister meaning in Gracken's pause which Max knew how to interpret.

''I don't believe she deceived you, Excellency!''

''When girls fall in love they're capable of anything—even treason.''

''She's loved before,'' said Max.

''And I can't forget that she's half American.''

''For that matter,'' said Max, forcing a laugh, ''I myself am part French; and you, Excellency—''

''—are of mixed blood; but I'm faithful to those who pay me. The faithless die. Suppose that we were to discover that this girl whom you appear to consider so highly herself had the papers, was now awaiting her lover safe, as she thinks, across the frontier! I'll show her that my arm is long."

"Your Excellency is right," whispered Max.

"And now to business," said Gracken. "I've given orders for every one on that boat who left for Switzerland last night to be followed and searched. There'll be no nonsense about it. You yourself will proceed immediately to Zurich by the way of Schaffhausen. I've got a passport for you. Get the paper out of that press over there."

Max stepped with alacrity over to a copying-press which stood on a plain deal table at the other side of the room. He spun the press open, returned with the paper which Gracken had requested him to get. It was an American passport, still moist. Gracken took the damp document and studied it acutely.

"The passport we found on the American when we fished him from the lake," he eluci-dated. "And it's genuine, too. I shouldn't have been surprised to discover that it was a fake. The fellow was capable of some such trick—leaving us a passport that would get us into trouble if we attempted to use it. The description fits you well enough—Samuel P.

Thomas, Wooster, Ohio, five-feet-eleven, light-brown hair—''

"And once in Zurich, Excellency?"

"You'll take charge of the entire squad of agents, unless—as I pray God they have been—the papers have already been recovered. In that event, you'll get them without delay and return immediately to Germany with them. The Emperor himself has his eye on us.'' Gracken whispered what followed: "The existence of those papers outside of the Empire is a menace to the dynasty."

Gracken and his assistant got to their feet. Gracken strolled over to a sunlit window. Out there were the wide railroad yards, and, beyond these, the melting breadth of the Lake of Constance. There was no hint in all this of the tragedy which had been enacted out there the night before, nor of the infinite tragedy which engulfed the world—not until far up in the clear sky and almost invisible there drifted a faint and microscopic Zeppelin, then a second, then a third.

"Not all the Zeppelins in the world will avail," whispered Gracken, "if those papers should, perhaps, reach the President of the United States!"

Max had followed his chief to the window.

"You can count on me," he said.

"Even to this extent," said Gracken. "If Operative Three-Thirty-Nine—otherwise, Miss Ruth Bancroft—is instrumental in getting these papers returned to Germany her life will be spared; if not"—Gracken confronted his aid —"you yourself will see that she is executed!"

A slight trembling took possession of Max. A slight pallor came into his face.

But he grimly saluted.

CHAPTER IX

OPERATIVE 339

THERE were about twenty passengers, besides Mrs. Nichols, on that boat that left Germany for the Swiss shore—a dozen Germans, four or five Swiss, a Spaniard, and a Brazilian and his wife. There must have been a degree of secret rejoicing, or at least of relief, among them. For the time being, Germany was not good to live in. They were out of it. But it is doubtful if any passenger on the boat had a spirit more tranquil than Mrs. Nichols' own.

The stewardess who had shown her to the tiny state-room bade her good-by with tears in her eyes. For, during the latter part of the run across the lake, the stewardess had discovered that here was some one to whom she could unburden her heart—about the death of Karl and the maiming of Adolph, and the slow sickness that was creeping over her sister's four young children.

72

"But—*ach, ja!*—Germany will win!"

"If you take an old piece of flannel," Mrs. Nichols suggested, "and bind it rather tightly about the youngest child's body I'm sure that he will get some relief."

"And keep it there?"

"Take it off in the evening and give his back a brisk rub—poor little dear! That is always good for anemic babies."

Papers of state? There was no occasion to think of papers of state when children were under discussion. Then there was even no Germany, no United States. Children were children, and mothers were mothers.

Personally, there was only one thing that worried Mrs. Nichols at all—and she wouldn't admit that this worried her greatly. But she was just a trifle short of money. It was going to take a little careful management to get to Vermont. This was especially so because of her limited wardrobe. She had given away all she could spare before leaving Stuttgart, so what she wore and what she had in her valise would have to last the journey through.

But she was not so badly equipped.

There was the dress she wore—a black alpaca and almost as good as new. She had never been hard on her clothing. It was true that her

bonnet was beginning to get a little shabby,
but no one expected travellers to put on style.
And there was her black lace cape. It had
given her years of royal good service and still
gave her a comfortable sense of being genteel
whenever she put it on.

Nor had she ever been a big eater. None of
her precious money would have to go for ex-
pensive meals in the restaurants. A roll and
a cup of coffee and a little fruit now and then!—
that was enough for any one. Old people didn't
have to eat so much, especially when they
weren't working. She was in a fever to get
to work at something or other. She didn't believe in idleness. As soon as she was in Switzerland, she would buy some thread and a crochet-needle and begin to make some lace.

Up between the twin glare of two white arc-
lamps the voyagers from the beleaguered Empire passed into the white and sickly radiance
of a custom-house.

Switzerland!

But it was three o'clock in the morning, with
a chill dampness in the air that made the dull
and haughty beauty who was the Brazilian's
wife draw more closely about her the gorgeous
furs she wore and made Mrs. Sylvia Nichols

more grateful than ever for her own service-
able cape of ribbon and lace.

This time, however, the examination was a
mere formality. Switzerland was like a rock
in the sea—an ocean of war; and those who
reached it were like shipwrecked sailors, not to
be submitted to search or inquisition any more
than other shipwrecked sailors were. The
health of the travellers was the important thing,
as a medical-major of the Swiss army explained
as he looked over the new arrivals with shrewd
eyes.

He called Mrs. Nichols "mother," when it
came her turn, and wished her a safe and pleasant voyage home.

A middle-aged customs-officer opened her
black valise and lifted this and that with hands
that were almost reverent—the clean handker-
chiefs, the neatly folded and delicately fragrant
linens, plain but hand-sewn, in perfect order.

Later on he entered the compartment with
her in the little train that was to carry the
passengers up toward Zurich. It appeared
that he had a cousin named Winder who had
emigrated to America ten years ago, and who
had made plenty of money, but had had trouble
with his wife; and the customs-officer wondered

if the lady knew anybody named Winder, and
if she ever did meet him—

To the amiable and not unpleasant music of
his speech Mrs. Nichols dozed.

It couldn't have been for long. The train
was still climbing slowly through tortuous darkness when she again opened her eyes. But her
sleep while it lasted must have been deep.

She awoke with the impression that she was
still telling the Swiss customs-man good-by,
only to discover that two other passengers had
already taken his place. One of these was a
heavy-set, low-browed man of forty or so, well
dressed enough but somehow rough and un-
couth. The impression was heightened by the
manifest bad humour he was in. The other
passenger was the one, however, who elicited
Mrs. Nichols' immediate sympathy and interest.

This other passenger was a young girl of
nineteen, perhaps, or possibly twenty; although
her youth was overcast by some suggestion of
age and experience very far beyond her years.
Also, she was a striking blonde, with that sort
of bold but fragile beauty that awakens at once
the lurking desire of men and the envious curiosity of most women.

Mrs. Nichols felt the curiosity when she first

glanced at the girl, but there was no envy in it. Rather it was sympathy.

She wondered if the girl could be married to the man at her side. She hoped not. The man was apparently finding fault with her, savagely, although he spoke in such a throaty undertone that Mrs. Nichols could hear no word of what he said. What most inspired her sympathy, though, was the fact that the girl looked as if she might be an American.

"I declare," said Mrs. Nichols aloud, "I must have been taking a nap!"

The man's ugly flow of speech came to a sudden stop. Both he and the girl stared over at her in the corner where she sat. The man's eyes were small and dark and sharp. They were like the eyes of a wild boar, with a hint of red in them even here in the none too brilliant light of the compartment. The girl's eyes were wide and blue, exquisitely arched by brows darker than her hair.

The girl was the first to respond to Mrs. Nichols' smile.

"Are you an American, dear?" Mrs. Nichols softly inquired.

Her whole desire had been to interrupt whatever it was the man was saying and protect the girl at least to that extent. The girl now re-

sponded with an odd little flash of eagerness.
"Yes."

She also had spoken English.

Now what, Mrs. Nichols wondered, could an
American girl be doing—riding in the cars at
this time of the night, in Switzerland, with a
man who looked like that? She still felt a certain curiosity as to whether the pair were married. But it was not just to satisfy her curiosity that she pursued her questioning. It was
a calm resolve to protect the girl further if
such protection should be needed. The girl
was so young that she could not be expected to
have much judgment of her own, and possibly
she had never had any one to advise her.

"What's your name, dear, if I may ask?"
Mrs. Nichols inquired.

From the man there came a throaty protest,
but the girl ignored him with a slight shrug of
her shoulders as she continued to smile. She
hesitated only an instant, reached her own decision.

"My name is Bancroft," she said—"Ruth
Bancroft!"

CHAPTER X

LOVE AND HATE

THEY were in that part of Switzerland where German is the exclusive speech, where hundreds of thousands of Germans live, and where German agents of one sort or another could circulate almost as freely as they could within the limits of the Fatherland itself. Mrs. Nichols was perfectly aware of all this. And it hadn't required the tragic death of young Samuel P. Thomas back there on the other shore of Constance to inform her of the extremes to which the spies of the Empire would go to repossess themselves of those papers which she now carried on her breast.

This knowledge was quickened—was flashed to the surface of her consciousness—when the girl pronounced her name.

"Ruth Bancroft!"

That was the name which had been mentioned by young Thomas himself in the course of that farewell interview. The girl was a spy. And the man with her must be a spy.

Yet neither now, nor in the midst of what immediately followed, did Mrs. Nichols feel alarmed.

The first sign that something was amiss came with a shock of brakes and a stoppage of the train so brutal that it might have been caused by a collision. Then in the comparative silence that followed there came a succession of feminine shrieks followed by a bellowing medley of discordant voices.

"*Gott!*" grunted the man at Miss Bancroft's side.

He hurled himself at the door of the compartment and was out into the night without more delay.

Miss Bancroft herself had shown a disposition to follow, but she evidently changed her mind, resumed her place with what appeared to be a little stroke of weakness. But this weakness lasted for an instant only. The man had left his overcoat behind him. The girl's eyes fell upon it. Yet again she hesitated. Then she seized the coat and thrust her hands into various pockets of it. From one pocket she drew a number of papers, from another she took a revolver.

All the time that she was doing this she had her eyes, so to speak, everywhere—on the door of the compartment by which the man had left, on the door opposite, on those tiny apertures which served as windows between this compartment and those adjoining. But most of all she looked at Mrs. Nichols. Finally she spoke.

"Don't be alarmed," she said. "I won't let any harm come to you. I wish I were out of it myself."

The revolver she had thrust into her handbag. The papers she had hastily scanned, one after the other, in tremulous haste and yet with a sort of lingering concentration, before returning them to the pocket whence she had taken them.

Meantime, there came evidence from outside the train as to the nature of what was going on out there. The same voice which had shrieked was now becoming coherent. The girl listened.

"There's been a robbery," she announced.

Officials of the train were running back and forth with a great swinging of lanterns and a growing hubbub as various passengers joined them. There was a strident whistle from the locomotive, a clanging of the bell, a huge sigh of compressed air.

"I hope no one was hurt," said Mrs. Nichols.

The girl gave her a quick look—of pleased surprise, one would have said at so naïve an expression.

"I think not."

"Did you hear who it was?" Mrs. Nichols asked.

"The wife of a rich Brazilian—they came over from Germany in the same boat with you—says that an armed robber stole her hand-baggage and her furs—right from her compartment—while she and her husband dozed."

"That is too bad," said Mrs. Nichols. "I suppose that some poor man was driven to it by hunger. There is an awful lot of misery in the world just now."

Miss Bancroft gave her a peculiar smile.

"I suppose you thought I was a robber myself when you saw me go through the pockets of that coat."

"No."

"You won't say anything?"

"Nothing—except that if I can help you in any way, dear—"

Still the smile that lingered on Miss Bancroft's young-old face, beautiful withal, was peculiar. She plumped herself down at Mrs. Nichols' side, took one of Mrs. Nichols' hands in her own.

It was at that moment that another dramatic touch was added to the events of the night. It wasn't much, perhaps, as events were then running in Europe. But this was in neatly governed Switzerland, against the sable background of the war, led up to by that surprising robbery which had just taken place. It befell in that instant of silence following the whistle from the locomotive, the jangle of the bell, and the gasp of the air-brakes. It was the bang of a revolver-shot!

Miss Bancroft gave a violent start; but Mrs. Nichols, looking at her, remained calm. Mrs. Nichols clung to the hand the girl had extended to her.

"And don't you be frightened, dear," Mrs. Nichols said.

"I—I've—got the jumps," the girl laughed, in an effort to be light.

The train, with a slight preliminary jerk, ground slowly into motion. The man with the eyes of a wild boar had not returned. His overcoat lay there on the upholstered bench on the other side of the compartment like something conscious—consciously deserted. The girl looked at this. The train began to pick up speed.

"We are living in a terrible period of the world," said Mrs. Nichols; "but we must never forget that God is with us."

The girl turned swiftly and looked at the old lady.

"Do you really believe that?" she asked with obvious surprise and curiosity.

"Oh, yes! And I've lived a long time, you know."

"But if you knew all that I know—if you'd been through some of the things I've been through!"

"Child," said Mrs. Nichols, "I couldn't have been much older than you when I was already a mother and a widow. It was war then—all fifes and tears, flags and bandages! I sent out the one splendid lover God had given me—"

Was it mere forgetfulness?—or was it some manifestation of the higher wisdom? Mrs. Nichols put her delicate fingers into the breast of her alpaca gown and brought out that precious packet of letters.

"—and God took him from me," Mrs. Nichols said. "I declare! The train is moving. Your husband must have—"

"That wasn't my husband," flared the girl.

"Oh, I didn't wish to be rude—"

"I hate him," said the girl. She whispered rapidly: "When I heard that revolver-shot just now, I wished—" She checked herself. Her eyes seized curiously on the packet of papers Mrs. Nichols held. "What are those?" she demanded with concentrated interest. "Did you bring those out of Germany?"

"Yes! I was just telling you. See! Two of these envelopes were sent to me from battlefields—one bringing me the last message from my husband, the other the last message from my only son. Both killed! Do you suppose, dear, that my old heart has not suffered all that your fresh young heart may have undergone?"

"There are things you don't understand," the girl murmured.

"It was all brought home to me last night," Mrs. Nichols went on, with gentle reminiscence, "when I saw a fine young American killed—"

The girl flashed upon her a startled glance.

"A young American killed! How?"

"Shot!—They shot him down—a score of them—"

"While he was trying to escape?"

"I think not," said Mrs. Nichols. "I guess he was merely trying to do his duty. He wasn't afraid—wasn't afraid to die—no more than I am—nor you will be, if the time ever comes."

The girl who had announced herself as Ruth Bancroft had been listening to all this with flashes of emotion. Now she was brilliantly hard. Again she was reflective. She had given a little gasp. She shuddered slightly. She was rigid.

"Oh, God!" she burst out briefly.

Her eyes flared at Mrs. Nichols, this time, with veiled desperation—just as some one, when trapped, might look for an avenue of escape.

"Ah, yes," Mrs. Nichols went on, softly, "and I know how that boy's mother will feel when she learns how he died. At first, she'll think that her own heart is broken, that she herself is dead. But Love will heal her, and Love will sustain her. I never say that God is Love. That's too hard to understand. I say that Love is God. For some of us poor souls don't seem to be able to know what God is. But where's the woman who doesn't know the sweetness and the majesty, the joy and the might of love!"

"Hate!" whispered the girl. "That's what I've known."

She was still reflecting, apparently, on the announcement of the American agent's death.

She must have heard enough previously to have suspected something of the kind. What Mrs. Nichols said had been mere confirmation. Now, it seemed as if all of those previously flashing and shifting moods of hers, found their expression in a gust of grief. She had no sooner made that declaration of hers about hate, rather than love, having been her portion, than her brilliant eyes became misty, and she collapsed against Mrs. Nichols' shoulder in a paroxysm of grief.

CHAPTER XI

BEFORE DAWN

TO any one aware of the nature of the papers now contained in those envelopes Mrs. Nichols had withdrawn from her bosom it would have meant a creep of most lurid distress. She had let the ribbon-bound packet fall to her lap, and there the girl herself picked it up. She continued to hold it as Mrs. Nichols comforted her.

Did Ruth Bancroft know? Did she suspect that here in her hands were those papers for which two mighty nations were contesting?— the prize upon winning which her own safety depended?

If so, she gave no sign of it. Her emotion dominated her—with that domination of emotion long pent up.

"Is your mother living, dear?"

Miss Bancroft shook her head.

"But you have plenty of friends?"

Mrs. Nichols spoke consolingly. Her hands

caressed the girl's pliant shoulders. And in the girl's own hands—convulsively nervous—was the packet with its flowered ribbon.

"I've never had friends even," Miss Bancroft wept.

"Ah, surely, dear—"

"One! One friend—unless—"

Mrs. Nichols took thought, giving the girl time to weep her grief away.

"Tell me all about it," she suggested. "Perhaps I can help you. No woman suffers what some other woman has not already suffered before her."

Miss Bancroft, under the influence of this persistent sympathy, at once so gentle and so sane, began to recover her self-possession. The packet of papers slipped from her own fingers, and then from her knees, as she drew a handkerchief from her handbag. As she did so, the revolver she had taken from the overcoat came for a moment into full view. It was apropos of this that she looked into the other's eyes with more trustfulness than had been there before.

"I told you that there were things you don't understand," she said, gustily, with an evident willingness to explain.

"I don't like to see a beautiful young girl like you—with a revolver in her possession.

Why don't you put it back? I shouldn't keep the ugly thing about me."

"You're not in danger," said the girl.

"Ah, but I am—and armed."

"How?"

"By faith!"

Miss Bancroft used the handkerchief she had taken from her bag to wipe her eyes. Thoughtfully she looked down at the revolver in the open bag. Thoughtfully still she brought from the bag a little silken purse containing a tiny mirror and a powder-puff. In the mirror she examined herself. She hastily touched the powder-puff to her dainty nose. All this was automatic. There was no lack of deference— or of reverence, even.

"Not for years—not since I can remember," she said, rapidly and smoothly, "have I heard any one speak as you have spoken to me. Love! Faith! The two words have almost gone out of my vocabulary. And yet," she added, with that characteristic touch of abstraction, "they do mean something to me as you used them. It makes me wonder—"

Her voice trailed off.

"They're words which mean the same for every one," said Mrs. Nichols.

The girl eyed her again, speculatively, almost

coldly, but concentrated on her own line of thought.

"I'm going to take you into my confidence," she said. "I'm not the young innocent you think I am. I wish I were. The robbery back there—that shot we heard—that man who was sitting here, and who may be dead now for all I know or care—these were all incidents of the same thing. I myself am an incident of that thing." She hesitated a moment longer. "Some one has taken certain papers out of Germany. I thought that boy they killed last night had them, but evidently not."

She paused with sudden recollection. She looked down. She saw the little packet of envelopes that had slipped to the cushion between herself and Mrs. Nichols. She picked it up. But Mrs. Nichols was listening with lively appreciation.

"So what will happen?" Mrs. Nichols asked.

"I don't know what will happen," Miss Bancroft answered, "except that nothing but a miracle will ever save the person who has them now—or me, if I'm not instrumental in getting them back."

"Do you mean—"

"Death," the girl replied. "You saw what they did to that boy last night."

"I thought you were an American," breathed Mrs. Nichols.

"Half American," the girl answered. "At least, so I've been told—that my mother was American. It's her name I use."

"And was she the friend—the one friend—you mentioned?"

The girl shook her head.

"That's a man—the nearest thing to a real man—in the whole hideous world I live in—a world of liars, assassins, traitors. There's a man by the name of Count Otto von Gracken at the head of it. Max—and I myself—might have been like other people if it hadn't been for Gracken. It's when I think of Gracken—and for the past four years at least he has made me think of him—that I doubt the meaning of those words you use."

She was becoming a trifle incoherent under the pressure of the feelings and memories she had no power adequately to express. With one of her quick reactions she regarded the packet of envelopes.

"Love!" she exclaimed, looking at it.

For the first time since the packet escaped from her possession, Mrs. Nichols also looked at the envelopes.

"Love is right," the old lady breathed with gentle conviction.

She made no move to take the papers from the girl. In her mind there must have still been echoing what the girl had said about nothing short of a miracle being able to save the successor to those other messengers who had been killed.

"It must be wonderful," the girl struggled on, "to have lived where you live—in a world where love and faith are realities."

"You could live there—if you would."

"It's too late!"

"You're so young! Why, child, your mother's country will receive you with open arms, blot out your past, teach you to look toward the future with a new hope. That's what America is for!"

"Too late, I tell you. They'd kill me! Kill me—just as they'll kill whoever it is has these papers we're after."

"But with God's help!"

"You almost make me believe," the girl panted, as she passed the precious packet back into Mrs. Nichols' hand.

She did it without so much as a glance. Her eyes, soft and luminous now, were on the slowly revolving, slowly emerging panorama of the strengthening dawn—broad surfaces of indigo, of paler blue, of heliotrope, then of pink—a pink, sky-soaring, unearthly peak which could already see the glory of the rising sun.

CHAPTER XII

UNDER HIS SHADOW

THERE was increasing evidence that Count Otto von Gracken's power was no more limited by the frontiers of the Empire which employed him than was that of one of his own powerful and equally secret wireless telegraph stations. As from the latter, so in fact from him, went the occult communications which meant life and death, success and failure, urgent questings and equally urgent commands.

These crossed frontiers as if frontiers did not exist, climbed mountains and descended into sheltered valleys, went whispering out to sea where certain lonely captains were the only ones who could understand, and still on and on, invisible and deft, to the Americas, to Asia and Africa, and all the scattered islands of the Seven Seas.

But the battles of superintelligence against superintelligence which go on day and night behind the firing-line also have their casualties—captured, killed and missing!

In other words, all of those secret messages which Gracken scattered so liberally over the earth did not fall exclusively into the hands of his own agents nor of those, even, who were merely friendly. Before six hours had elapsed, various of these messages had already been picked up and decoded, thus bringing to the knowledge of the world the fact that certain papers of first importance to an imperial dynasty were new *en route*.

Whither?

That depended on who happened to have them.

Who was this person?

That was a question which not only Count Otto von Gracken himself but various other personalities most ardently desired to know.

This much was known:

A young American had almost succeeded in getting out of the Empire with the papers in his possession. He was efficiently killed. The papers were gone.

The Intelligence Departments of England, France and Italy entered the game at Count von Gracken's unsuspected invitation. Over in America certain other departments had begun a vigil every empty, succeeding hour of which was going to mean increased suspense.

But to Mrs. Sylvia Nichols the world was beautiful and calm.

She was not dismayed even by the fact that all the passengers who had crossed from Germany the night before by way of the Lake of Constance were being detained in Zurich. The order was only natural, perhaps. Certain unusual events had marked the journey, events which demanded investigation. How long the investigation would last was something the authorities were either unwilling or unable to divulge.

In any case, worry would be futile—futile and wicked.

Moreover, Mrs. Nichols was no longer so friendless and alone as she had been the night before at the dark terminus in Germany. In the great *Bahnhof* of the Swiss city she had waited and dozed, for the fatigue of the past twenty-four hours—and the past twenty-four months, for that matter—was beginning to weigh upon her. But Ruth Bancroft had come to her assistance.

Not far from the *Bahnhof* was a little old house in a little old street.

"And here," said Miss Bancroft, "you'll

have a chance to wash up and rest. The lady who owns the place is a friend of mine. She'll be delighted to take you in."

"God bless you, child," said Mrs. Nichols; "but I could take a cat-nap right here in the station."

"It may be night before you get permission to move on," Miss Bancroft replied. "It's going to take longer than that for some of the others, but I'll look out for you." She affectionately embraced the old lady, smiled down at her. "You know, I can be a witness for you."

The house to which Miss Bancroft had brought the unsuspected messenger was quaint and beautiful—half-timbered and sharply gabled, with immaculate curtains at the leaded windows and flowering geraniums on the window-sills. Miss Bancroft's friend was scarcely less attractive—one of those fawn-skinned women from the south of Germany who still look as their ancestors might have looked before the Romans came.

She showed Mrs. Nichols into a bed-chamber as immaculate as those window-curtains were, and assured her with a warmth that couldn't be doubted that there was neither pleasure nor honor in this world she coveted quite so much

as rendering some small service to the gracious
friend of the gracious *Fräulein*.

There was a Bible in this room, and when
Mrs. Nichols was alone she looked at this with
a heart-hunger greater than any physical hunger she had ever known. Her own Bible she
had been forced to leave behind her in Stuttgart—as printed matter capable of being con-
verted to untoward purposes. Her satisfaction
became all the greater when she picked up the
Bible and discovered that it was English.

She turned first to that portion of the Scrip-
tures which had already occurred to her—that
passage wherein it is related how One Other
with a great message to deliver, when He also
was surrounded by enemies bent on his destruc-
tion. . . .

*Passing through the midst of them went His
way.*

She turned to that great Epistle to the He-
brews:

*By faith they passed through the Red Sea
. . . . through faith escaped the edge of the
sword . . . turned to flight the armies of the
aliens . . .*

She had bought a spool of thread and a little
bone crochet needle. She had been idle so long
that she hated to lose any more time, even if

she was sleepy. She sat down in a comfortable chair and started the lace she intended to make.

Marjorie was going to need a lot of lace. Young mothers always did. And, oh, if it would only be a boy!

Her white head nodded forward. Her hands dropped into her lap. And who could have told what visions did not unroll just then in the little Swiss chamber—Chickamauga, perhaps; and the palms and the pink, yellow and blue stuccoes of Cuba; or the cool green hills and the white houses and church-steeples of Vermont; and through and over these ever the hurrying columns, like driven clouds, of devoted young men following a flag. It was the flag of the Union—a flag that leaned perpetually forward to the charge!

But not throughout the rest of the house did such perfect peace prevail. That ferment of which Count Otto von Gracken was the center and the author had begun to work.

The fawn-skinned woman from the South of Germany was receiving visitors. The visitors were many, both men and women. They came singly. They dropped in casually. One or two might have been professional men. One or two might have been artisans. But most of them were persons of ordinary appearance, plain and respectable. And most of them lingered for merely a minute or two.

Had any one asked them, they had just called to pay their dues to the Benefit Society. That was all.

But some of the callers remained. And these wondered where *he* was and why *he* didn't come. And then, at last, *he* came.

It was Gracken's chief assistant, Mr. Max.

CHAPTER XIII

CROSS-CURRENTS

THE other visitors already assembled there showed the newcomer a degree of deference. No less deferent was the woman of the house. She bowed. She fluttered. She smiled and pushed forward a chair. But Max was in an unsmiling mood. He didn't scowl precisely, but he looked about him with an intensity which the others found disconcerting.

"What news?" he snapped.

"None, as yet. Perhaps, now, at any minute—"

"*Recht!*" It was no time for idle speculations. There fell a moment of silence accented by a far drubbing. Guard-mount somewhere! Even Switzerland was mobolised. Max snarled: "Where's Three-Thirty-Nine?"

"Sleeping," said the woman of the house. "Shall I tell her you are here?"

"No!"

"As your Excellency—"

"Has she made any report?"

"None: she came here with an old lady—"

"Hah!"

"A stranger—"

Max delivered himself of an impatient gesture to command silence.

"I've heard about that," he announced. "You others," he snapped, "be about your business. The orders are to get those papers and place them in my hands without delay. No half measures! I'll keep in touch with Great Headquarters." He turned to the fawn-skinned woman with a quiet disregard of the others as they disappeared. "Where did you put this old lady?"

"In the front room on the second floor."

She gave him the information with a smile that was not altogether official; but Max was, outwardly at least, impervious.

"And Three-Thirty-Nine?" he pursued.

"The room to the rear."

Her smile persisted. There was an appeal in her eyes.

"Thanks," said Max. "You stay here."

Alone he mounted the narrow, heavily framed stairs to the second floor. It was evident that he was perfectly familiar with the arrangement of the house. In the upper hall he

stopped and listened, first bending his attention on the room at the front where the stranger
was, then on a door at the rear. To the latter
door he made his way silently. He found it un-
locked. He thrust it slowly open.

The room was heavily timbered. The light
that entered it did so subdued through a leaded
window, yet it revealed a certain disorder. A
woman's clothing was scattered over a nut-
wood chest. There was a small but cumbrous
and heavily carved wooden bed, and on this,
curled up in a pink peignoir, her fair hair loose
and dishevelled, lay Ruth Bancroft asleep.

Max closed the door behind him.

But he did not lock it. Perhaps he knew that
the fawn-skinned woman would be listening,
would come creeping up—as she did, half a
minute later—to watch and listen—listen with
a concentrated passion of interest which had
nothing to do with questions of state.

Miss Bancroft opened her eyes. She started
up. Something of her alarm left her when she
recognised her intruder.

"Well?" she asked.

"Well?" he echoed softly. He made, however, no effort to conceal his ill nature.

Miss Bancroft's pink lips parted in a yawn
which she only partially stifled. She scowled.

She swung her stockinged feet to the floor and sat there contemplating him.

"What did you do"—he drawled this much of the question, snapped out the rest of it—*"with those papers?"*

Miss Bancroft looked at him unflinchingly for a good thirty seconds in silence. Then she shifted her gaze, shook her heavy hair around over her shoulder and proceeded leisurely to replait it.

"Your humour is delicious," she said.

"I asked you a question."

She shrugged a glistening shoulder.

The interlude was sufficient to give Max time to master his emotions. To one even less observant than Ruth Bancroft it would have been apparent that these emotions were complex—jealousy, rage, longing, bafflement, admiration, the impulse to kill.

"Ruth—"

"That is better!"

"You were with that young American—"

"How do you know?"

"Gracken has been watching you."

"It was at his orders."

"And you—"

Miss Bancroft faced him again. The semblance of mockery had left her by this time.

"Don't say it, Max," she warned, softly. "There are some things that not even that swine can make me do!"

"Swine! Be careful!"

"I'll call him that! Gracken told me that he wouldn't have this boy killed. I might have known! If I only had! I would have got the papers, but neither you nor he would ever have seen them."

"Quiet! Do you value your life?"

"No!"

Max made a movement of despair.

"If you had secured these papers for me— your American would now be safe."

"You're as bad as the rest of them."

"I had nothing to do with killing the boy, but I would have killed him if I thought—"

"I tell you—" Miss Bancroft quavered passionately.

She also left her sentence uncompleted. She and Max looked at each other eye to eye. Gradually a better understanding was establishing itself between them despite the broken and stony nature of their communication hitherto.

Outside the door the fawn-skinned woman decided that she had heard about as much as she dared listen to. And, anyway, she was not altogether unrelieved. Silently she withdrew.

Max changed the subject.

"What do you mean," he pursued, "by bringing a stranger to this house?"

"She was merely an old American lady in need of a friend," Miss Bancroft retorted. "When I learned that Gracken had killed that other American I decided to do something to pay off the debt I owe to my conscience. I can't forget that I'm half American myself. That's why I took her in."

"But she's been in Germany."

"What's that got to do with it?"

"And last night left it—by the same boat this other American tried to take. Perhaps she—"

"Don't be a fool!"

"But if even you yourself are open to suspicion! Those papers are still in existence. I want them. I intend to get them. And let me tell you this—"

"You can save me the heroics," Miss Bancroft remarked. She sat there a while longer immersed in thought. She abandoned her recent mood altogether. "Max," she said, "there's something else in this world than lies and treachery. I'm sick of it all. I could scream."

Max lit a cigarette. He strolled over to the leaded window and stood there in the deep embrasure looking out. There was a tiny garden there, and the garden was giving a little festival all its own in honour of the return of Spring. It had spread a fresh green carpet on the floor, hung up a million lanterns more or less of pink and green, perfumed all this sagaciously in a way to touch the imagination of butterfly, bird and man.

Quite possibly, Max himself was conscious of all this, but his eyes travelled to a house beyond the garden, then to a shuttered window of this house.

The shutter trembled. Between the slats of it he saw a flitting gleam of eyes.

"Spies, spies," he muttered. "Spies against spies."

Miss Bancroft had used the time to resume a portion of her raiment. She bade Max follow her. They crossed the hall. Miss Bancroft herself slowly opened the door of Mrs. Nichols' room.

They paused there, looking in.

Mrs. Nichols was still seated in her easy chair. Her head was back. There was a faint flush on her rose-petal cheek, and her modest bosom slowly rose and fell.

Herr Max breathed an exclamation. It was one that was habitual with him. Yet also it happened to be the German word for that very thing which his eyes now saw:

"Mutter!"

CHAPTER XIV

IN ALIEN HANDS

THERE for a time Max seemed to waver. He looked at that little old American lady seated there, while into the whole appearance of him there came an odd look of reminiscence, of regret, of some softer sentiment, and yet all this still touched with bitterness. Then his long training began to reassert itself. He turned to Miss Bancroft.

She made a movement of intercession, but against this Max manifestly hardened himself.

"You—you," he breathed stormily; "you make me forget!"

"I make you remember," she answered calmly, still looking up at him with that pleading look in her eyes.

"Forget duty," he whispered; "and remember—what?"

"Love!"

Something of that steel-and-acid charge he had brought with him from Count Otto von

Gracken had gone out of Max, but his discipline conquered. It was a triumph which was not immediate but it was sure.

"Have you questioned her?" he whispered.

The girl nodded.

"Searched her?"

"No!"

"Then I'll have it done."

"Max!"

"Stand back! I'm not going to hurt her."

Miss Bancroft did shrink back, with her hand on her heart, as Max rapped with his knuckles on the open door. But all the time that Max was in that room the girl stood just outside— listening, ready again to intercede or protect, compelled to do this by some emotion which she herself perhaps could not have analysed.

At the knock on the door Mrs. Nichols had opened her eyes. At the opening of her eyes she smiled. Max, with a degree of politeness, and yet with a greater degree of authority, stepped into the room.

"I hope that you are comfortable," he murmured, in English.

"Thank you," Mrs. Nichols replied. "Won't you sit down?"

She was telling herself that she liked the

young man's looks. It was only natural that one traveller should visit another.

As for Max, he had cast one sharp glance about the room. He graciously accepted Mrs. Nichols' invitation, gave her a cool but not unfriendly survey.

"Troublous times," he remarked.

"I like to think—it's all for the best."

"War!" droned Max. "This city is full of refugees—sick and wounded—the hateful and suspicious—murderers and spies!"

"Poor souls!"

"It is of that I wish to speak," Max calmly proceeded. With no great appearance of doing so he was dissecting Mrs. Nichols with his eyes. She had picked up her crochet and was placidly at work. "I happen to have heard," he went on, "that—certain papers—have got out of Germany. You've lived in Germany?"

"For the past two years."

"Then, perhaps, you know something about conditions over there—almost every one has—how the Emperor receives certain private reports intended for his eyes alone. It appears that three of these papers have gone astray—and that they are turning heaven and earth to get them back."

Mrs. Nichols' quiet concentration on her crochet-work permitted him to proceed with that visual dissection of his. But now she looked up at him.

"I know what war is," she remarked softly.

"Then you know to what extremes the agents of the Empire are likely to go in their efforts to get the missing documents back. It won't be a question of those papers alone, but of any papers which have been carried—by any one— out of Germany. I thought I'd better warn you. Have you any papers?"

"I have these," Mrs. Nichols said.

Max sat rigidly still. Mrs. Nichols had dropped her lace in her lap. There was a fondness in her eyes—something transcendental. Without haste, without nervousness, she brought the packet from her bosom and considered it. Into Max's eyes there came a gleam of eagerness.

"What are those?" he demanded quietly.

"The dearest papers in the world," she answered. "That's why I carry them next to my heart." She gave him an alert look. She smiled. There again crept into her delicate cheek that hint of a flush. "These—these are the documents of the greatest love in the world!"

"And what is this greatest love?"

As Max asked this question he may have been conscious that Ruth Bancroft was listening at the door.

"What is this greatest love?"

"Love of country," Mrs. Nichols said.

"So—o!"

"Son, how old are you, may I ask?"

"Twenty-six," said Max, with a flash of recollection. That was the age mentioned in the passport of Samuel P. Thomas.

"At that age," said Mrs. Nichols with a glow of enthusiasm, "my husband—we'd only been married a few months—and when I think of his chivalry and devotion!—was already consecrated—"

"You mean—"

"Dead!—dead on the altar!—but, oh, so living!—in the spirit of all who are true-hearted!"

Max had reached over and taken the packet of papers. He studied it, as if with his eyes he could have torn the envelopes apart, devoured their contents. Mrs. Nichols, unprotesting, leaned forward.

"He was killed in our Civil War, as you will see by the date on that upper envelope. I suppose that no man—especially if he is young—can quite fathom the feeling in a woman's heart. Remember that, when some girl gives you her heart. But I did learn, after a time, to thank God that David died as he did; and that in the same way my other David—that was our son—"

"Him also!"

"Yes, you see that second envelope. I had brought the boy up so like his father that when the next call came, nothing would satisfy him but that he also go—where the danger was, and the duty, and the glory! He fell—with an imcompleted letter in his pocket. It was to me, and every time I read it he seems all the more alive—as if he were still intending to finish it—and would, some day."

There was a suppressed but raucous eruption of speech from the lower hallway, a tread of heavy boots on the wooden stairs. Max started up and listened. There followed a brief interchange at the door—Miss Bancroft and a man as yet unseen speaking together in German. Max was on his feet. He still had Mrs. Nichols' precious packet in his hand as he strode to the door.

The newcomer was the man who had been in the train with Ruth Bancroft the night before. His small and boarish eyes appeared more bloodshot than ever. One of his hands was wrapped up in fresh bandages.

"What is it?" asked Max.

The other saluted awkwardly with his wounded hand.

"You're wanted, immediately, at headquarters," he replied. His unlovely eyes travelled past Max to the interior of the room. They fastened on Mrs. Nichols. She had resumed her crochet work. "What is she doing here?" he muttered. "She was in the train last night when that *Schweinhund* took a shot at me."

Then, suddenly, his eyes had fallen to the papers Max held in his hand. Miss Bancroft also was looking at those papers. Now Max looked at them. He was not without a certain proud dignity. He gave the other man a scornful glance. He gave Ruth Bancroft a look of challenge.

He slipped the papers into his pocket.

CHAPTER XV

IN CASE OF ACCIDENT

MRS. NICHOLS, alone in her room but with the door still open, was aware of what was going on out there in the hall. She gave no outward sign of it. Visibly all she did was to continue her fancy work. The crochet-needle was nimble in her placid hands. Her face was serene. Once she lifted her face and let her mild eyes rest on space in general.

But who could have told, unless possessed of some extra sense, that inside of her there had come one of those sudden attacks which try the souls of women and men?

Yet that was the case.

Gone! Those papers were gone from her possession. Had she done right? Was there still time to get them back? Or was it too late? Could she make an appeal? And if she did, would they listen to it? Cry out! Her heart was in a tumult. She hadn't lived without pain. Both physical and spiritual torture had racked her often enough. But there had never been an attack like this. Other times she had not cried out, except in the depths of her heart. Would her strength suffice her now?

She looped the thread about the hook of the needle. She counted seven. She had never made this particular design before. Once started, it was simpler than the old kind. She could get ahead with it faster, once she was on the steamer bound for America.

"—*in vain the net is spread*—"

Her eyes had come back to the thread. The thread itself had whispered back the old words to her brain.

Outside, in the hallway, Max, with those papers in his pocket, confronted the man with the small and bloodshot eyes. The man was sullen, but Max easily dominated him, not only because of a superior station but because of some indefinable moral supremacy.

"How long are they going to want me?" Max inquired.

The other shrugged a cumbrous shoulder. "The orders are from Number One himself."

"Von Gracken!"

"And urgent!—that is all I know."

"*Zu Befehl!*"

The other turned. As he did so, Max involuntarily met the eyes of the girl. Involuntarily he answered the appeal in her eyes.

"What is it?" he snapped.

"Max!"

Ruth said no more until the heavy feet of the Human Boar were clattering down the stairs, but she had put a hand on Max's arm. The appeal was still in her blue eyes, but it was not the appeal of one who was afraid. Nonetheless Max persisted in a step or two toward the stairs.

"I have no time," he informed her brusquely. "I'll see you when I come back."

"When you come back!" she whispered bitterly.

"Yes."

"You may never come back!"

"Right enough!"

He had reached the head of the stairs. There Ruth stopped him.

"There may be an accident," she said with soft intensity. "I don't have to tell you that. You've seen how many of us fall. So have I."

Max permitted himself a joyless laugh.

"What are you trying to do—frighten me?"

"Those papers!" flared Ruth.

"Well, I intend to get them!"

"I mean—those you already have."

It was a longish interval before Max could seize the import of her words. He was mildly astonished.

"Do you mean—these?"

There was a slight smile on his face as he drew out the packet he had received from Mrs. Nichols and contemplated it.

"Yes," breathed Ruth.

"You women!" Max exclaimed. "I merely want these so that I can be sure. The only way I can be sure is to have them analysed. Now— *auf Wiedersehen!*"

His foot was on the stair. He smiled again. In spite of his impatience he took Ruth's hand, brushed a kiss across the fingertips.

"Max," she persisted, "is there nothing sacred?"

Something in her voice made him turn back. He remounted to the upper level where Ruth stood. Impulsively he gave her a little embrace. He seemed to be responding to some lure about her which he hadn't known before. He began to murmur in French.

"*Sapristi!* You women! We think we know you! We discover we don't! We think you're bankrupt. Your resources are barely touched!"

As if to bear out his philosophising Ruth hung her fair head. There was a girlish soft-

ness about her—a childlike quality forsooth—
that was new to Max. He could stand her
fierceness. He could stand her contempt. He
was perfectly familiar with her brilliancy and
her courage. He was suddenly aware that here
was a Ruth Bancroft he might have imagined,
might have longed for, but which hitherto he
had never seen. He paused where he was. He
embraced her again. She surrendered to his
embrace. When she looked up at him her eyes
were moist.

"What do you mean?" he whispered.

She gazed into his eyes for several seconds
before she spoke.

"There's something else in this life besides
Gracken and Gracken's orders," she whispered.
"That's what I mean. That's what I meant
when I spoke to you a while ago about that dear
old guest of mine—in there! Max, you heard
what she said about those papers—about the
love in her heart. What if something should
happen to you—so that she didn't get those
papers back?"

"So it was—love of her—and not love of
me?" Max mused with characteristic masculine
jealousy.

"Equally love of you," Ruth corrected him
soberly.

"I don't understand."

But he was beginning to understand—as he continued to look into her face, continued to take note of her yielding strength. Man persists in looking for his ideal in the one girl, the one woman, and the recognition of that ideal is invariably stronger than passion.

"You heard what she said—'the dearest papers in the world'—'the greatest love in the world'—'love of country!' These are the papers that you are going to contaminate. This is the thing you are going to contaminate. Max —not only for her sake, and the sake of what she represents, but—for your sake, give them back to her!"

"Ruth, when you look at me like that, speak to me like that—you make me almost regret—"

Ruth did not smile.

It was by an obvious effort that Max looked away. It was toward the stairs, whither Gracken's orders were impelling him.

"Give them back to her," Ruth was whispering.

"Perhaps," said Max slowly, as he re-entered the room, "you had better let me keep these papers for you until you are safe from those German agents I was speaking about."

If Max had had eyes in the back of his head he could not have been better aware of the fact that Ruth Bancroft was now standing openly at the door looking in at him—at him and Mrs. Nichols.

"That is very kind of you," said Mrs. Nichols gently. "I am apt to be a little forgetful, and if anything should happen to them—"

Max once again turned and stepped to the door. He had murmured something about coming back without delay. He saw a look in Ruth Bancroft's eyes. Possibly it recalled to him something that Mrs. Nichols had just said about the unfathomable feeling that women sometimes know. Again Max hesitated. He stopped. He about-faced.

"What you've just told me," he said with swift intensity, "is very beautiful. A little later—then you can let me keep your papers for you—if that is necessary. Now I am going somewhere—and there may be an accident. Accident!—men getting shot!—happening all the time!"

He took the papers from his pocket.

"I hope that nothing like that will happen to you," said Mrs. Nichols looking up at him with maternal warmth.

Max was still hesitant.

"I feel that it would do me good," he said, softly and urgently, "if I had your blessing."

Whatever his nationality, it was an Old World school to which he had been bred—a school as old as the lineage of Abraham. He bent his knee. On one knee he knelt and bowed his head. On his head he felt the caress of her hand, then the infinitely more thrilling and somehow divine caress of Sylvia Nichols' face.

Max did not leave on that errand of his with the promptness that German discipline is supposed to exact. He had closed the door of the old American lady's room behind him. In the russet twilight of the hall he lingered face to face with Ruth Bancroft.

"Those papers?" she whispered.

"I couldn't desecrate them," he replied. "I left them in her blessed lap."

"I knew—"

"What?"

"—that your heart was right."

They stood there very close to each other looking into each other's eyes. "And remember that," a voice was repeating in the young man's brain, "when some girl gives you her heart." Max's arms stole out. Miss Bancroft's face was still uplifted to his as his arms drew her closer yet.

"What are papers of state," he murmured, "compared to papers like those!" He was clarifying his own thought rather than attempting an argument to convince the other. Her he didn't have to convince. "What does anything in the world matter—if but such feeling as hers be kept alive!"

Miss Bancroft failed to find the words to express immediately what she had to express.

"It is as if she were from another world," she faltered.

"Our own—some day—God grant!" whispered Max.

CHAPTER XVI

"MADAME, LA FRANCE!"

ARRESTS, strange hold-ups, perhaps a murder mystery or two; a churning excitement underneath the ordered activity of the Swiss metropolis and the outlying cantons! All this, and still no trace of the missing papers!

"We'll have to go on into France," said Max, later in the day. "The search is fully organised here."

Ruth Bancroft looked into his eyes.

"And I?"

"You'll go with me," he whispered huskily.

"Max, what are you holding back from me?"

"Nothing! You can help me."

"Max!"

He succeeded in facing her.

"Gracken doesn't trust you," he confided steadily. "He wants you killed. He blames you for not having got the papers from the American, Thomas."

126

Max looked away again with a sharp access of bitterness.

"I didn't even know his name," Miss Bancroft answered. "I couldn't—couldn't do what Gracken ordered," she continued, while a slow flush came into her cheeks. "Max, I tell you, it was on your account."

Max evidently allowed his thoughts to flow for an interval without making an effort to express them.

"Well, Thomas was his name," he said—"Samuel P. Thomas. I have reason not to forget. It's under his passport that I'll have to cross the next frontier."

"It could carry you—into America," Miss Bancroft breathed.

The full significance of her suggestion came only gradually to Max. He had an impulse, so one would have said, to take her more deeply into his confidence than he had already done. But he flinched. He mastered himself.

"When comes peace," he answered huskily.

He said this in French, but it was not surprising. Three languages he spoke as any native might have spoken them—German, French and English. It was in English that Miss Bancroft next addressed him.

"That dear old American lady—she's made me think—"

Herr Max broke in upon her.

"It is of her I would speak. I'm having a motor take us over to the French frontier. There's no time to lose on trains. We'll take her with us—if you can get her to go. With her along there'll be less suspicion—we'll be Americans all!"

"If it were only so," Miss Bancroft whispered.

Again Herr Max looked at her with that queer expression of his—an expression half fierceness, half longing, and both repressed.

"In any case," said Max, "you'll tell her that I am American. But you needn't tell her the name I'm travelling under until that becomes absolutely necessary. You—never—can —tell!"

Switzerland is a region of splendid roads. There is one such road particularly which runs from Zurich down toward Bern and thence to the French frontier. One of the master-roads of the world it is. South of it, across the rounded meadows and wooded slopes, lift range on range the highlands of Lucerne and the Ber-

nese Oberland. Closer, to the north, runs the
overwhelming pageant of the Juras.

No wonder that forever afterward, always
when Mrs. Sylvia Nichols heard heaven mentioned, it called up a vision of this part of the
world as she saw it that day and the next.

She had accepted that invitation of Ruth
Bancroft and the supposed American with both
gladness and gratitude; for she began to see
that without some sort of help her journey
home was going to be a long and tedious one.
Once away from Zurich she would have to stop
in Bern to have her passport once more put
in order. And then; would she be able to get
a train without losing another night, another
day? It wasn't herself she worried about. It
was the papers. Perhaps the President was
waiting for them even now. She couldn't keep
him waiting. But with the offer of a motor
ride her difficulties disappeared. In her heart
she prayed. In her heart she sang a Psalm!

Then they were out on the road—in that powerful motor-car on a perfect day, with the
mountains marching past in all their solemn
grandeur, personal, huge, and dim, arrayed in
ethereal uniforms of purple and green, azure
dissolved in glistening white, and the white

itself veiled with the substance of the ineffable sky!

The very air was as pure as God Himself had made it!

Herself—O prophetic thought!—no longer little and old, but borne along as on the wings of an archangel!

She knew that Ruth Bancroft was a German spy. But she couldn't regard her as dangerous. Concerning the young man she merely put her faith in God. For, although she may have suspected that both of them were part of that desperate and deadly combination designed to regain possession of those papers she herself held hidden in her bosom, how could she be afraid when these two were showing themselves so friendly!

Love would help her.

Love had preserved her these eighty years.

And these two were Love's agents. Weren't they giving her just such aid as she needed? The car was going much faster than any train could have gone. It was much more comfortable. And it meant an economy, too.

She had done her best to get Miss Bancroft and her friend to accept the amount of her railroad-ticket. But, no; they wouldn't think of it.

It was that larger aspect of the run, however, which gradually took possession of her as the speeding car swayed gently over the padded landscape—an aspect including an immense exhilaration, a fathomless peace and joy. She had a sense of the imminence of her Maker—of sharing in the possession of all Knowledge and all Power.

How like life this was!—where every one was a messenger of sorts!—carrying a message which was secret from the world!—which enemies would destroy!—a message received from the hand of an unknown and which had, nevertheless, to be carried as a sacred trust to the journey's end, there to be delivered, unbetrayed, into the final keeping of the Commander-in-Chief!

And so she winged along!

The spectacle might have been humorous if it hadn't been for the hovering tragedy of it—this little old lady thus being speeded on her way by the chief agent of the redoubtable Count Otto von Gracken. And even so, Mrs. Nichols took it none too seriously.

She found the two German spies delightful company, and that's the truth. They stirred her great expectations—but these expectations were on their own account. She could see them

happily married, both of them showing the
sterling qualities she was sure they possessed—
or would possess as soon as the war was over.
Hadn't she seen similar miracles worked at
the close of the Civil War?

Deftly and gently, more by looks than by
words, she conveyed these expectations of hers
to the two young people throughout the run.
She told Herr Max that she was glad that he
was an American—gladder yet that he was
going back to America now, unless, perchance,
he chose to remain and fight for England or
France.

For Herr Max, as he himself had suggested,
had been introduced to her as an American.
She hadn't caught his name. Nor had she inquired about his family or his business. This
was wartime, when men were not to be too
closely questioned save by those in authority.

The three of them were seated on the wide
rear seat of the heavy tonneau. In front there
was a chauffeur who evidently knew his business and yet who, from time to time, turned off
from the main road to ask questions at isolated
houses. So, for all the speed, the run was also
leisurely—leisurely enough for Mrs. Nichols
to doze again and dream and send her spirit

circling to the mountain-tops and over and beyond them.

It was in the early afternoon of the second
day after her getting out of Germany that Mrs.
Nichols awoke from one of these numerous,
dreamy naps. There had been a long stop at
Bern, while the passports were being viséd, so
she wasn't tired. Her mood, in fact, was more
subtly cordial than ever. It was as if a change
had come over the atmosphere. There was a
warmth at her heart as well. And she sat there
for possibly a dozen seconds—half asleep, half
awake—before she discovered that she was
alone in the car.

Off to one side of the road there was a plain,
whitewashed house of plastered brick. To the
other side, further along, was another building
of the same sort but immensely larger. There
were a number of men about—all of them in a
queer grey-green uniform—and almost as many
rangy dogs that kept trotting about.

The whole scene was supremely peaceful. It
was quiet, too, almost to the point of absolute
silence. No dog barked. No man spoke in a
tone that was audible. The only sound that insisted on being heard was the jerky, irregular,
muted *clink-clong* of a cowbell from some dis-

tant pasture, and this merely intensified the atmosphere of Sabbath calm and safety.

An old man appeared. He was very old—trudging along with an old straw hat on his white hair, otherwise in the dress of a peasant, with wooden shoes on his feet. He was smoking a pipe and pushing an empty wheelbarrow. He came alongside the automobile.

"I beg pardon," said Mrs. Nichols.

Almost unconsciously she had spoken English. But, whether the old peasant had understood her or not, he had stopped. He did it with a fine dignity. He put down the handles of his barrow. He removed his pipe from his mouth and his hat from his head. He bowed low.

Mrs. Nichols thought she had never seen a finer face. The man must have been as old as she was herself. She loved such gallantry—among equals.

"Can you tell me," Mrs. Nichols asked, "what place this is?"

The old man lifted his face. His eyes were bright blue.

"*Madame*," he said, "*c'est la France!*"

CHAPTER XVII

AMONG FRIENDS

ALMOST at the same instant a breeze came over the brow of a hill and shook out wistfully the folds of a flag that had been clinging to a high staff. The very colours of it were enough to send a thrill to her heart. It was as if all those premonitions of hers, those communings of hers with the Almighty, and her exalted spiritual flights—things that neither she nor any one else, perhaps, could have expressed in words—now found expression in that single banner of blue and white and red.

"Our colours, too," she whispered to herself.

There was a smile on her lips. There was a dimness on her eyes. There was a pain at her heart. All these things seemed to have entered into the consciousness of the old French peasant. He did not look at her. Hat still in hand he bowed again. He trundled silently away. And then Sylvia Nichols could have wept, had she permitted herself to do so. But she wouldn't permit it.

"If I start that," she told herself, "I'd never stop."

For she was telling herself also that the beautiful France was old, and grievously hurt. But would France weep? Ah, no! France would hold back her tears even though it killed her! France had lost a husband. France had lost a son. France was now risking her life.

"Like me," whispered Sylvia Nichols. And again: "And I'll try to act like you."

Thus showing her strength—as the widow of a soldier and the mother of a soldier should, especially in the presence of a greater and yet more chastened grief—she prepared herself for that new ordeal which she knew couldn't be long delayed.

In fact, it was coming now. A group of military had appeared at the door of the smaller building. She saw that the building bore the simple inscription, "*Douane*"—meaning that it was the custom-house. One of the military group, a youngish officer, approached. He was sober but polite. He wished to know if madame would give herself the trouble to alight and follow him. Madame was only too willing to obey.

At least, Mrs. Nichols said so. She spoke

French in the same pure but hesitant way that was hers when she was speaking German.

But the young officer, always so sober and yet so polite, helped her to get down from the car.

"Your friends," he said, "are already undergoing their examination."

Mrs. Nichols felt a slight touch of sickness. Now were they indeed her friends? And was she doing right in permitting the representatives of this country she loved almost as much as America to think that they were her friends? The girl at least was a German spy. And yet of the girl, somehow, she felt sure. But how about the man? She didn't know what to say.

"They've been very kind to me," she volunteered.

And as she said it she turned her thoughts inward, took counsel of her spirit. Inwardly she said: "I was told that he was an American." But to this her spirit retorted: "Why, then, this doubt that assails you? Why the intuition that something is wrong?"

Little and old, and more bent than usual—under that invisible burden of thought—she accompanied the officer into the custom-house. At the door she paused, a little faint. But as she did so, looking straight ahead of her into the somewhat gloomy interior of the place, she saw something that heartened her as would have heartened her the face of a life-long friend. And yet it was nothing but a lithograph. It was cheap. It wasn't even framed. The colours were crude. But still it had been tacked up here in this French outpost—"Washington Crossing the Delaware!"

Friends? Weren't all these people her friends?

"Have you, perhaps," asked the young officer curiously, "any papers to declare?"

"Yes, *monsieur*."

She was in the presence of Washington now.

The young officer had turned sharply, was looking at her with eyes that, while respectful, were as keen as those of a hawk. Hawklike indeed they were—the eyes of the new-old France, the France of the Revolution, the France of to-day.

"*Tiens!*" he breathed slowly.

They had come into a sort of outer office. There were a couple of elderly military clerks softly wrangling over certain books at a desk. Just inside one of the several doors a stout matron, young and strong, dressed in black, and wearing a brassard on her left arm to indicate that she also was of the customs service, waited for whatever orders might be given her.

But, this time, Mrs. Nichols was able to smile at the soldier. She felt almost as if Washington over there could hear her—was listening now. Washington would understand.

"What are these papers—which you have to declare?" the young officer slowly asked.

The two elderly clerks dropped what else they were doing and looked up. The stout young matron moved over from her place near the door. It was as if at that second mention of papers a little electric current had run through the place, touched every one in it with a crisping interest.

"They're—love-letters," Sylvia Nichols answered, softly.

She drew out the packet from her breast.

"Des lettres—d'amour!"

France was still France, after all. The two elderly clerks came nearer. So did the matron. By some sort of magic the news spread. Appeared a captain of gendarmes, then a civilian with grey whiskers and a black calotte. Awed and tender! That was their attitude.

"Des lettres d'amour!"

Love-letters! At the frontier, on her way from Germany to America, had appeared a little old lady. No, romance was not dead. When the little old lady was questioned about the papers she had to declare, what was her answer? Love-letters, *pardi!*

The young officer took the packet of three envelopes which Mrs. Nichols extended to him. He was slightly embarrassed. But duty was duty. From certain headquarters had come word that papers of the most vital importance to modern history were somewhere in circulation and that the utmost efforts be made to find them. He looked at the packet. He looked at Mrs. Nichols. Any one could see with half an eye that he was going to follow instructions—slip the ribbon, open the envelopes, assure himself of what they contained.

Mrs. Nichols stood before him. Possibly she shrank a little. She felt all those eyes upon her. But she was mild. The only expression in her face was one of gentle expectancy.

The young officer made a preliminary movement of fumbling with the ribbon.

At that moment a door opened and from some interior room a superior officer came out—superior and older; with a white mustache and white imperial, in fact, identifying him with the Second Empire; yet ruddy and brisk, alert of step and eye.

"What's this?" he questioned briefly.

He was instantly to the fore, as the others fell back respectfully to give him passage. He carried authority. He was inclined to be curt.

Then his agile faculties had taken in the situation. Into that fierce military eye of his had come a gleam.

"Madame says they're love-letters," some one explained.

The elderly officer took the packet of envelopes from his subordinate's hand. The gleam in his eyes became a smile. The smile was for Sylvia Nichols as he looked from the packet of papers to her, then back again.

"But certainly," he said softly; "and why not?"

"The colonel understands," said Mrs. Nichols.

"Assuredly!"

The colonel's appreciation was growing. He also eyed the packet tenderly. As one who does something unconsciously he brought it to his military nose and breathed the fragrance of it.

"Ah!" he murmured. And then: "The pretty ribbon—flowered and old—like the souvenir of an ancient love! *Madame, mes compliments!*" But the colonel was no less the soldier. He had remarked the date on that en-

velope which was uppermost. *"Tiens!"* he
cried; "1863!"

"From my husband—"

"A soldier?"

"Killed in action, at Chickamauga."

"Chickamauga! *Sapristi!* Why, madame,
myself I was there, attached as observer to the
staff of General Rosecrans—a brave soldier, a
gallant gentleman!" He turned to his subordinate. "Look into this lady's eyes," he exclaimed, impetuously, "and tell me whether she
is enemy or friend." He didn't wait for the
younger man's pronouncement. "Madame, I
have the honour—"

He handed the precious packet back to her.

CHAPTER XVIII

PAROLE

SO seldom are the joys and triumphs of this life unalloyed! Peace comes only after the payment of the terrible cost. The triumph has its ranking wound—a secret doubt, a remorse only half-suffocated, a knowledge that the triumph itself is still incomplete. Human joy is a mere poor *Little Red Riding Hood,* out in the woods, and at her side stalks always at least one spectral wolf.

"*—Monsieur Samuel P. Thomas—*"

The name fell upon her hearing. Like a bomb it fell upon her consciousness, entrenched though she was in all that friendliness and honour which surrounded Mrs. Nichols at that moment.

Through the door by which the colonel himself had come some half-dozen other officers and civilians connected with the post had made their appearance. In the midst of them was Mrs. Nichols' supposed American friend of the automobile. It was he who had been addressed by that name which Mrs. Nichols had last heard from the real owner's lips on the German shore of Constance.

Mrs. Nichols was still smiling as she spoke to the old French colonel. She had told him about her husband in the army of Rosecrans. She had told him about her son in the army of Roosevelt and Wood.

And all gallantry was he—strong in the tradition of Franco-American friendship and the worldwide acceptance, madame, of the transcendence of American womanhood.

But even while he thus spoke, and she spoke and also smiled, and still held those fateful papers now safely in her hand, it was of young Samuel P. Thomas she thought, the boy of Wooster, Ohio, who had died so gladly in a far country—not for America only; but for France as well, and England, and the world! Could she now deprive his sacrifice of even a shred of its value by allowing a German spy to use that name?

Her flashing intuition which by the law of compensation so often becomes stronger as the ordinary faculties begin to fail through age completed her knowledge of what had taken place. Thomas dead, the enemy had found his passport, were utilising it now to forward the business of one of their spies. This was that spy.

With him she had come riding into France. Him she had permitted them to believe to be her friend.

Fresh air was the immediate need.

"I'm feeling a trifle faint," she confessed to the old colonel. "I shall be all right in a moment if you'll permit me to step out doors."

She had but to command.

Outside the white building she cast a glance in the direction of the motor-car. It was as she had suspected. Ruth Bancroft had already passed the inspection, was seated in the car over there now waiting for the others to come. Miss Bancroft, seeing her, raised her hand in a cheery greeting.

Mrs. Nichols tried to smile, but smiling was becoming instantly more difficult. Once more, just back of her, she heard the supposed American being addressed as M. Thomas—M. Samuel P. Thomas. There could be no doubt about it. The French, as is their way when dealing with an unfamiliar foreign name, were taking no chances with the customary elisions. They were pronouncing the name in full.

"What shall I do?"

It was a spring of speech in the depths of her being.

The question was not so simple as it might have appeared. To some extent she felt responsible for the presence here on French soil of both these spies. Yet to both she felt an odd gratitude even now. To denounce them would be to have them shot.

Nor was this yet all.

Suppose she did denounce them; wouldn't that entail explanations of all her own conduct? Those explanations she would have been ready and glad to give had the consequences of them been limited to herself. Not she had anything to fear, not even death. But death would not suffice. Nothing would suffice but life—life and liberty—to get these papers of hers to Washington.

That she had promised; and, even if she hadn't promised, these papers somehow were essential to the country's good.

Quite abruptly she turned, she faced the supposed American.

"May I speak to you a moment?"

She couldn't have been gentler. There was no hint about her at all as to what was going on in her heart and brain. Herr Max was equally debonair.

"How can I serve you?" he smilingly asked.

They had stepped a little distance apart from the others. Max had taken his hat from his head with a characteristic politeness. The sun glistened on his blond hair. The queer fancy occurred to Mrs. Nichols that to him also had come some breath of warmth and rejuvenation such as she had known on, crossing the French frontier. She hesitated a moment longer as she looked up at him. That moment was long enough for her to have a vision of him standing blindfolded against a wall, a firing-squad drawn up in front of him.

"You're not Samuel P. Thomas," she accused him softly.

He blanched, but he continued to smile.

"I beg your pardon—"

"You're not Samuel P. Thomas," she repeated. She spoke just as softly as ever, but a touch of desperation had come into her tone. Impulsively she added: "I saw Samuel P. Thomas die. I love and honour him—as I love and honour America—love and honour France!"

The most momentous passages of human speech are seldom ranted. The conversation was little more than a murmur.

"That was the name in the passport," said

Max. "I had to use it. There was none other."

"You're not an American."

"No."

"You're employed by Germany."

He looked unhappy, but in the look there was no negation.

"A spy!"

"What do you expect me to do?"

"Go back—go back now before it is too late."

"I can't."

"You must."

"There is something you don't understand."

"I understand the work of a spy—a spy's fate if he is caught."

"You wouldn't denounce me," whispered Max.

"Can't you see that I'm giving you a chance for your life? There is the frontier. I wish it might have been otherwise. I was grateful to you—had expectations—"

"If I tell you," said Max, "that everything is all right! If I tell you that I mean no harm to France! Quick! Those officers over there will begin to suspect. See! Miss Bancroft wonders what we are talking about."

Mrs. Nichols slowly shook her head. Her heart was swelling with grief and joy, pain and alleviation. She was doing right and she was paying the cost of doing right.

"What is your country?" she asked.

Max gave her a look of bitter anguish.

"This is no time for a boy like you to be without a country," she hurried on. "If it's Germany, go back and fight for it there, like the man I know you to be. Don't stay here and get yourself killed like a spy. I should have known. I was partly responsible. Don't put this fresh burden on my old heart."

"Would you have me killed?"

"Rather than see France suffer, yes!—as God is our Judge."

It was a surprising thing, what followed. For a moment or two longer Max had continued to look down at Mrs. Nichols with a sort of surging intentness. There was admiration in his look. There was pain in it. There was bafflement. Suddenly he turned toward the group of officers who had remained just outside the door of the custom-house.

"Oh, Colonel Junot, if you please!"

He had actually taken a step in the direction of those who Mrs. Nichols had reason to believe were this young man's deadly enemies, but Colonel Junot—he who had been so gallant in the return of the papers—himself stepped forward. He and Max met. Between them there was a swiftly whispered interchange. The colonel's face went grave. Together they rejoined Mrs. Nichols. It was the colonel who spoke.

"Madame," he said, with dignity, "you, as a mother of one soldier and the wife of another, understand that there are military exigencies. I honour you all the more for the stand you have just taken. Will you permit this young man to proceed—as Samuel P. Thomas—on my parole that he will do no harm to France—"

"Nor to America—or any of her allies—"

"Madame, on my word of honour!"

There was something about all this that Mrs. Nichols could not understand. Only this could she understand, that of Colonel Junot's devotion to his country there could not—could not!—possibly be any doubt.

Perhaps she murmured something to this effect. Max, saluting, turned away. Colonel Junot, soliciting the honour as he might have done in the florid days of the Second Empire, gallantly saluted Sylvia Nichols' hand. *Adieu, madame! Adieu!!*

CHAPTER XIX

TIES OF BLOOD

THERE was that time when Max received some mysterious word that carried him and his passengers north, and still further north, until once more at a pause in the late afternoon there came to all of them that grunt of the unknown—a hiccough of the universe, the paroxysms of something nameless and incredibly huge. And the agony of the beast was endless. Great guns again! And, in spite of all that it meant, that *umph! umph! umph-umph!* filled them all with the intoxication of excitement.

Whatever it was, that word Max had received from Colonel Junot, it permitted him free circulation—across guarded bridges, through zones scarred line on line with man-deep trenches, along barracks whence came a breath of iodoform and frightening silence.

But the sky was beautiful. Between the waiting trenches which—please God!—they would never have to use, the peasants were at work,

the tender green of early barley showed itself.
The night came on. While the west was still
old rose, touched up with flame, the friendly
moon appeared in the darker east. And so,
most likely, will come the end of the world—
that mirage of perfect peace and through it all
some muffled, mighty tread, the hand of the Almighty knocking at the door.

So what mattereth it the end of the world if
He be there!

Never had the thoughts of Mrs. Nichols been
so high and clear. Gentle she had been, and
meek, and brave in the face of adversity.

But the mood she had brought with her over
from Switzerland was something that she had
never known before—not even in the days of
the Civil War, nor of the Spanish War when
word first came that her only son was dead.
Then, as the night deepened, she began to understand. The shadows were coming up about
her like a garment, and this garment was the
robe of France. The warmth she felt, and the
passion, and the tenderness, and the high fear-
lessness—these were of the breath and the
blood of France.

France! France! France!

She could have chanted it. Old as she was,

there ran in her veins an indescribable current of youth, and song, and defiance.

"I'll take my message to the President," she said. "Oh, now I know that I shall; for France, what things are impossible to the God that created thee!"

It happened at some nameless little station on a railroad line that a sentinel stopped the motor-car in which Max, Ruth Bancroft and Mrs. Nichols rode. He ordered Max to alight. He summoned a guard. A patrol came up. Then also the girl and Mrs. Nichols were requested to get down. All this happened in the darkness. There was not so much as a lantern discernible.

After an interval Mrs. Nichols was taken into a gloomy little waiting-room, and there she remained alone. She was not frightened. Everything was going to be all right. There was some light here—not much, but enough. She could have worked in the dark anyway. She brought out her crochet. The little band of lace was growing. She ought to have quite a bit of it completed by the time she arrived home in Vermont, and she knew how Marjorie would appreciate it.

"Grandmother made this—in wartime—in France!"

Ruth Bancroft entered, while a soldier stood guard at the open door.

"You are to go on to Paris by train," she said. "It isn't far. The train is expected to be here shortly."

"And you, dear?"

"I'm not permitted to answer questions. I can tell you, though, that everything is all right. There is no time to lose. Listen! The first boat that you can get back to the United States leaves Corunna, Spain, a week from to-day. Try to take it." She cast a quick look in the direction of the soldier at the door. "I shall try to be there, too."

A moment, and she was kissing Mrs. Nichols —kissing her good-by, one might have feared For, when the girl was gone, Mrs. Nichols felt a tear on her cheek, and she was almost absolutely sure that it was not her own.

Gone! But where? Had the identity of the girl been discovered?

And the young man! What had happened to him? Had he encountered some power greater and less benign than that of the old colonel who had been his protector at the frontier?

An enigma! But wasn't all life an enigma? Why else should those appear out of the unknown who win our interest, our love, only to disappear again—as these had done?—as so many had done before them!

Mrs. Nichols, with the memory of other wartimes still strong upon her did not attempt to question the young soldier who remained on guard at the door. She was rested. Paris was not far away. In Paris she would have much to do, for it was no easy thing to arrange, unassisted, for that sailing in Spain. Yet, wasn't this France?—even now, in the night!—in the midst of war!

She resumed her crochet.

A young officer came in. He met her friendly look with a friendly look of his own. He came over and sat down beside her. With a "Permit me, madame," he picked up the bit of lace she had completed. His lean, bronzed, face softened still more.

"*Joli*," he mused.

And he and Mrs. Nichols began to talk about lace—Valenciennes and Irish crochet, point-de-Venise, Mechlin mesh and Brussels mesh. He told her things about lace of which she had never known or dreamed, spoke with an enthusiasm, a science and a delicacy which quite carried her away. For he himself was a lace-maker, it appeared, and his forefathers had been lace-makers right back through the centuries.

He was describing a certain historic wedding-veil, wherein orange-blossoms and stars were powdered over a ground of incredible *vrai réseau*, when he stopped, sprang up with a swift salute, was gone.

There came the rumbling murmur of a train.

Mrs. Nichols dropped her crochet back into her black valise. The sentinel at the door, whatever his duty there, let her pass unchallenged. Into the station the train came whimpering and groaning like a wounded dinosaur. It was only then that Mrs. Nichols discovered that it was not the train itself that whimpered and groaned. It was a hospital train—a mother-dinosaur coming back from the battle-line up there with her stricken young.

The lace-maker with the fighting face appeared.

"Don't be frightened," he said. "They've transported me twice in a train like this. The pharmacist has consented to take you in. Come with me!"

Like that she came to Paris. The whole world was helping her.

But in Paris, in spite of this atmosphere of occult aid which surrounded her, delay followed

delay, day followed day—while still she waited
and prayed and did her best to expedite matters—prayed and knitted and dreamed in the little French *pension* where she had stopped
twenty years ago and where Mme. Marcin, the
landlady, still held forth not so greatly changed
—while great Paris revolved and throbbed
about them, once more become the master-
wheel in the mills of the gods, solemn and joyful, predestined, smooth-running, superhuman
and magnificent. Paris! It was the heart of
the universe.

It was an atmosphere of heroism, perfect
faith and a fore-knowledge of results, yet with
the hue of tragedy about it, that transmuted
the gold which was Sylvia Nichols into something finer still.

Otherwise, no woman of her age, after the
fatigues to which she had already been submitted, could have stood as she stood it that
weary ride in the slow cars that carried her
subsequently, away from Paris, forward on the
next stage of her mission. For, as a rule, those
cars were filled with soldiers. They were
muddy. Some of them were caked with mud
that was red. Dead weary they were, too, with
a weariness that was as yet too great for sleep
—shocked nerves which called for laughter

and speech. But in the eyes of these boys Mrs.
Nichols recognised a spirit which was her
own—something which also was finer than
gold.

The boys themselves she seemed to recognise. Right out of the miraculous and terrible
years of her own youth they came. They had
long hair and long beards. Their language was
potent. There was a look of wonder in their
eyes. Back from the winepress they were
going home. But return again!

"*Ah, Dieu!*"

How could a man stay away when there was
a chance to fight!

The train rolled into the last village of
France. It was Hendaye, late in the afternoon.
The setting sun flamed the Bidassoa into fluent
rubies. And just beyond the river was Spain.

CHAPTER XX

BONDS OF SORROW

OUT of Germany, through Switzerland, through France! A thousand, or ten thousand, spies intent as never before on securing those papers which had disappeared but which were known still to exist! Human life become as a mere breath on a window-pane!

Wireless messages had crossed and recrossed the Atlantic. Not in Germany alone was it ascertained that the leaders of the Great Republic waited—waited—waited for those papers which were known to have been last in the possession of a young agent named Thomas. It was even known that out in Wooster, Ohio, an elderly woman, in a small frame-cottage with a flower-garden back of it, also waited—in vain—for word from that youth, while she planted her jonquils and watched her tulips bloom.

And gradually, perhaps, the scattered inter-

est began to concentrate on that certain other
old lady, Mrs. Sylvia Nichols.

There had been just so many travelers from
the direction of the German frontier. Some
of these had been killed and searched. Others
had been trailed and robbed. Among the spies
themselves there must have been a higher mortality than usual. Promise there was, moreover, that higher yet would be the mortality if
the papers were not recovered.

And what if they had already been copied,
photographed, shown to the hostile chiefs?

Not yet! But it may happen any day. Hurry
up, you sleuth-hounds! Run down the quarry!
Tear him—or her—to shreds! There has been
cunning and treachery somewhere. Show
greater cunning and treachery of your own!

The Spanish town across the river was Irun.
Here was another custom-house. The passengers were many. And so also were—who
knows?—the spies and secret agents of the German Empire. And where these were numerous,
would there be any dearth of those as well who
worked secretly, keenly, desperately, for England and France? Add to these the agents of
Spain itself. There was an ambushed army of
them all.

To this army, by divers channels, had arrived

information that those precious papers were coming this way.

Get them!

Mrs. Nichols glimpsed this secret army with the eyes of her spirit. Her spirit rode in a battleplane, so to speak—high up where the air was thin and pure, where heaven was close and earth was distant, whence she could see things no human eye could discern.

What was that feeling which came to her, soaring at these altitudes—a feeling that she was not alone, that she was accompanied ever by a shining whiteness, a mystic gentleness?

"But He passing through the midst of them went His way!"

Her very poverty had become to her an element of thanksgiving. She was shod with sandals. She was taking with her no extra coat. So had the miracle-workers always gone.

So poor she was that almost she might have been permitted to pass through the Spanish custom-house without inquiry at all. For a long time she stood apart. It was a somewhat elderly Spaniard of a courtly demeanour who finally proceeded to her examination. That demeanour of his, however, had its counterpart in his exalted and impassioned devotion to duty.

"Has the señora any papers to declare?"
He had asked his question in English. Very
solemn he was. So Don Quixote might have
conducted himself had he been an inspector of
customs. He surveyed the little old American
lady with a sort of sad detachment. "I would
save the señora the inconvenience of search."

Mrs. Nichols, her eyes upon him, cautiously
but gently, possibly wondering if he was aware
of her silent prayer, once more took the papers
from her breast. She knew it now. They had
become her breath of life. Take them from her
and she would die. Not she could return to
America without them. America! She dared
not think how remote America still was, the
barriers that still intervened.

Into the sad and haughty eyes of the Spaniard had come a faint gleam. It would have
been a gleam of hope in the eyes of any other
man. But the Spaniard was as a man in whom
hope was not.

His hand, she noticed, was lean and aristocratic—like his face. He took the papers.

That Spaniard was poor. God only knows
what guerdon had not been promised to him
who should be so fortunate as to secure those
papers for which that secret army had been
mobilised! Who can blame him if his aristo-

cratic hand trembled somewhat as it received the packet? Or who can tell what mad hope flamed up behind that lean Quixotic mask of his?

He burst out with a question in Spanish. He repeated himself in English:

"What—what are these?"

Spain and America had been enemies in 1898. The fact was uppermost in Sylvia Nichols' mind. She wanted to say something to the effect that Colonel Roosevelt himself had praised the Spaniards, that so had her son. That was the thought that was uppermost, but from the deeper depths her spirit cried—

"De profundis clamavi ad te, Domine!"

But the Spaniard had surveyed that first envelope with a preliminary doubt suffusing his avid curiosity. He turned to the next, always without disturbing the ribbon which held the envelopes together. He looked at that which was written in the corner. His haughtiness was disintegrating more rapidly than ever.

"Cuba!" he faltered.

He pronounced it "Koo-ba!" He repeated the word.

"Santiago!" he murmured. He seemed to feel that such a display of emotion in the presence of a stranger was unseemly. With an im-

pulse to apologise he explained: "Pardon,
señora; but it was there I had the—the honour!
—to lose my son."

"You also!" responded Mrs. Nichols.

The look in her face completed her meaning.
It was a look which was not lost on the old
Spanish gentleman.

"We parents—"

"—understand," she said.

"Señora, pardon me," the Spaniard went on.
He brought the second envelope reverently to
his own lips. He allowed the three envelopes
to slip back into their former position. He
touched the flowered ribbon back into place.
"He was my only son—my boy who was lost
over there. His mother—and I are growing
old—"

He passed the packet of papers back to Mrs.
Nichols just as the French colonel had done.

"And may I have the great honour," he
asked, gently and grandly, "of escorting you to
your train?"

He himself picked up the black valise he had
already examined. Deferently he escorted her
through the custom-house and to the terminus
of Spain's great Northern Railway—while they
talked of Cuba, of the boys who had fallen

there, both American and Spaniard, to the ultimate betterment of the world.

Señora Sylvia Nichols! Señor Don Juan de
la Rosa!

They had introduced themselves to each
other; for now it was as if there was a bond between them—a bond not only of blood, but also
of tears, a libation on the common altar.

"Yea," said Sylvia Nichols in her heart, as
she listened to the Spaniard, "thus often are
men unknowingly servants of the Lord!"

The thought was still formulating itself in
her mind as she looked across the crowded terminal and saw some one whom she instantly
recognised—some one with immensely broad
shoulders, some one who walked with a stiff-
ness in one of his legs yet who was almost mechanically efficient, mechanically superior to
sentiment or mistake: Gracken!—Count Otto
von Gracken!—chief of the German spy sys-
tem.

CHAPTER XXI

SET TO MUSIC

ROCKS that rise rough and grey straight out of the blue water of a land-locked harbour; houses as shimmering and solid as if they had been carved from the rock, clustering along the waterfront and crowded along the hills above, all as delicately coloured in yellows, pinks, and blues, as if the weather had done the work and taken centuries about it; overhead a fleckless sky the same colour as the sea; a shifting breeze, salt and tepid, save in the immediate vicinity of the town, where the saltiness is enhanced by the additional fragrances of garlic and fried olive-oil, strong red wine and fresh sardines!

That is Corunna.

They still play guitars in Corunna. The men of the place have the same concentrated vigour for love and hate and adventure as their ancestors had when the Great Armada lay out there —out there where only the Spanish liner *San*

166

Carlos now lies, with her red and yellow flag painted hugely on her sides, ready to sail for the United States.

The fishing fleet, with buff and russet sails, glides in. The night comes on. Altogether Spanish, the *San Carlos* tranquilly smokes and waits—as the horizons fade, the revolving light at the harbour entrance takes up its nightly task, as the town comes twinkling out of the thickening darkness with ten thousand lesser lights and in the sky the stars softly and mysteriously emerge.

A man in a flat-brimmed Spanish hat and a flowing cape passed through one of the narrow streets near the waterfront. He entered a dark doorway and mounted a flight of stone steps to the second floor. There, he tapped on a door in a particular way. The door was opened a few inches to the rattling of a chain.

"Ruth!"

"Max," cried the girl.

She dropped the chain and opened the door. Max entered. They swiftly embraced each other.

"I was afraid that you wouldn't get here," she exclaimed.

Max was busy making the door fast again.

He got the chain into place. He turned to follow her.

"I was afraid of the same thing," he said, lightly.

They passed on through the large, barely furnished, brick-floored room and came out onto a balcony that overlooked the harbour.

"Have you seen Gracken?" she asked.

"I haven't seen him, but I've been in communication with him. He's coming on the express—will be here within half an hour."

"That will give us a chance to take the boat."

Max shook his head.

"I can't go," he answered. He put his arm about Ruth as if to forestall the protest. "Ruth, you understand. This is still war. If I had secured those papers, then I might have felt free to go—if only for a while—to see that you are safe."

As yet, Ruth was too overcome for speech. Down in the street a gipsy installed himself under a gas-lamp and slowly began to strum on his guitar. Now and then the man let out a shred of song—a sort of minor quaver, haunting and weird. He sang only when some one passed, and as yet the promenaders in this part of the street were not numerous.

"That old American lady, Mrs. Nichols—

she's coming on the same train,'' said Max. ''I got word from one of our people at Irun. He seemed to be under the impression that she might have the papers after all.''

''Oh, Max,'' quavered Miss Bancroft, ''I can't—can't go without you!''

''So you'll have at least Mrs. Nichols on board with you. If I'm not mistaken she'll need some sort of protection. She could have none better than yours. Even if there is no reason to suspect her, Gracken, or one of his men, would not hesitate to—to—''

Miss Bancroft turned her face to his shoulder. She was not crying. But there was a tenseness and a stillness about her which expressed grief even more than tears could have done.

''I might have known,'' the girl resumed, after an interval, ''that this happiness I looked forward to was too much—more than I deserved.'' The Spanish gipsy crooned his plaint, strummed his minor chords. ''You said that you hated this life you were leading—just as I have come to hate it. You said that Mrs. Nichols had given you a new outlook. Have you forgotten?''

''Ruth, there are two things I shall never

forget—no, three. One of them is the old lady
herself. The other is you.''

''And the third?''

Max did not answer the question immediately. He brought his face close to the girl's
fragrant head. He himself set sail there for
a space on the wings of emotion—circling up
and up on a widening spiral—wider yet—while
the earth dropped away beneath him. He was
taking Ruth with him. They were spirits only—
lighter than bees, and as strong on the wing.

Did the gipsy know what was going on up
there on the balcony? One would have said so.
One would have said that the gipsy knew even
that this was no ordinary tryst. Into his strum-
ming and his crooning there crept a keener,
wilder note—a note of yearning otherwise inexpressible.

Right up through the ages had come that
note, refined and polished by all the craving
that all the successive generations of gipsys had
ever felt.

To such music Max soared his flight and returned to earth again.

''You mustn't think that this is the end of
life,'' he was murmuring. ''Even so, we have
learned what life is—for we have learned what
love is, Ruth, you and I—have learned it to-

gether from that blessed old saint of an American. God is good. It would take a God who was good to have conceived her and created her and kept her alive for the world's inspiration. And you! Ruth! Ruth! Now we know—don't we, *mon ange d'amour?*—that our future is sure, whatever might happen! We know that even if we are separated, that separation will be only temporary!"

His exaltation was such that there had crept a note of prophecy into his voice. The incessant, barely heard music from the street accentuated this.

"What was that third thing?" Ruth persisted.

It was as if Max were listening to something more distant than the sounds from the street below, as if he saw something infinitely further away than the slowly flashing light at the harbour-mouth. He was facing north. Up there lay the bloody marches of Europe. Up there was that mightier music to which he had seen the regiments die.

"And that other thing?" Miss Bancroft whispered.

"Duty! Plain, old-fashioned duty!" His arm tightened about her. He pressed his face against her fragrant head. He closed his eyes.

Then he was the man again. "You go on—to your country. Later on, I'll join you there."

"When?"

"When I get those papers, or, at least, find out what has become of them."

Miss Bancroft was evidently in the midst of a struggle. As is usual when such a struggle takes place in a strong nature it did not translate itself readily into words.

"But if you don't get those papers?" she faltered.

"I'll get them!"

"But if you don't?'

"I'll get them—or die!"

Through Miss Bancroft's lithe and supple frame there ran a swift tremour.

"Not that!" she whispered.

As for Max, absorbed though he was in the emotions of the interview he was not unconscious of that struggle which was going on inside of the girl. There was a repression and thoughtfulness about her. While her breast heaved he knew that her mind was at work.

"Do you suppose," he whispered, slowly and steadily, "that Mrs. Nichols—really has—those papers—after all?"

The room back of them was unlighted. Such light as reached them came only from the street-lamp where the beggar stood and the dimmer radiance of the harbour. Max's eyes may have deceived him, but it seemed as if the girl's colour slowly receded from her face. The gipsy softly wailed and strummed.

"No!"

Her monosyllable was barely audible.

"In that case," said Max, softly, "I have an idea of my own as to where they might be found."

"Where?"

But Max wouldn't tell her. Instead, he gave minute instructions as to what the girl now had to do. She was to meet Mrs. Nichols and take her to a certain point of the sea-wall where a boat would be waiting. The owner of this boat could be trusted. There Max himself would come to tell them good-by. They were to wait until the steamer's second parting whistle.

"But if you haven't come then?" Ruth whispered.

"I'll be all right."

"But how shall I know?"

"What is that thing the old lady told you about faith?"

In the street below the Spanish gipsy quavered again into his doleful chant. With loose strings his old guitar throbbed a minor.

The man and the girl on the balcony kissed each other.

One of the most tragic old towns in Spain, and therefore in the world, is Corunna. And yet even tragedy is acceptable if it be touched up with a glint of romance, a colour of daring, a glamour of weird music under the Spanish stars. So much for the man.

But as Ruth Bancroft eventually closed the door on Max, she felt as if her heart would break.

CHAPTER XXII

AT THE SECOND WHISTLE

A S Max came out into the street that followed the waterfront the Spanish gipsy
evidently decided that this was not a good place
to woo fortune. He slung his guitar behind
him. He ambled off in the direction that Max
had taken. Max paused. They met where the
shadows were thick. They talked about divers
things, chiefly in an undertone so low that not
any one could have heard even when passing
close to where they stood.

But on leaving Max, the gipsy moved off at
a pace faster than that habitual to his kind.
Presently, he came to a place where a boat was
tied to the mole, and to the man in charge of
this boat the gipsy spoke. The boatman cast
loose his craft. He cranked its tiny engine and
chugged away. It was he who eventually received two passengers for the San Carlos at a
place previously agreed upon.

Thus the night swallowed up gipsy and boat-

man and allowed Count Otto von Gracken's first
assistant liberty to go and meet his chief at the
arrival of the train from Irun. On Gracken,
moreover, Max was concentrating all his attention. They met just outside the railroad station.

"What news?" the chief inquired.

"Important."

"The papers?"

"Yes."

They walked away together. Half an hour
later found them in a café where, apparently,
they both had friends. The café, like all other
places of any importance in the *Pescaderia*—
or lower town—was itself not far from the port.
At last, in from the port—on the breeze that
was at once salt and yet delicately flavored with
garlic and wine—there came the tremulous bel-
low of a ship's siren.

"I'll wait no longer," said Gracken curtly.
He surveyed Max with his placid but cunning
eyes. "The first thing you know the girl will
be getting away without my seeing her again.
You've kept her out of my sight long enough."

Max showed no resentment. He was merely
sober.

"*Recht!*"

"And I won't let her get away even now if

I think she's crooked," said Gracken. "I didn't come all the way down here to Spain for my health."

Max was silent.

The friends which both he and Gracken seemed to have in this café likewise decided to leave about this time, but Max and Gracken were alone as they stepped out into the night. They were alone when they came into that narrow street through which Max had previously passed, alone as they went up the stone steps.

"I told her to leave the door open," said Max.

He had taken a step in advance, Gracken stomping along just back of him. They were both abreast of the door. Max had pushed it open. He turned to his chief.

"Go on in," he said.

Gracken stood absolutely motionless. There was no motion about him whatsoever except the slow rise and fall of his mammoth chest.

"Go on in," whispered Max. "You've guessed it. I've got you covered."

"You—you—"

"Be careful what you say."

"We'll call it off," suggested Gracken.

They were standing there at the head of the

stairs, with that open door at their side, as tense and hostile as two rival tigers at the mouth of a cave.

"Call it off!"

"Strike a truce," Gracken pursued, cautious and smooth. "I'll see that you get what you want—"

"I want those papers."

The sweat was pouring from the faces of both of them, but that was almost the sole outward symptom of excitement which either displayed. They spoke softly, but in that close look they were getting of each other each must have seen that time for speech was brief.

"I haven't got them," said Gracken, now speaking slowly and with an effort. "But I know where they are."

"Where?"

"Mrs. Sylvia Nichols—the old American—"

"*Nom de Dieu!*"

"She fooled us all. No! Not all! Ruth Bancroft also knew!"

"You lie!"

"It stings you, does it? Well, for your satisfaction, and for mine, I can tell you that—I have taken means—to bag them both." Gracken must have noticed that start Max gave. He repeated—"to bag them both!"

Max fought for self-recovery.

"You've got the papers yourself," he declared.

But in Max's mind there was a dawning comprehension of that struggle which he was aware had taken place a little while ago in Ruth Bancroft's heart. With the comprehension his own heart fled to her. He felt a curious gratitude, which Gracken could not have understood.

"So the girl deceived you!" Gracken taunted.

Events had been proceeding so swiftly and smoothly, so superficially normal, that none could have guessed that Death had joined the party. Perhaps both Max and Gracken knew. For a long time both had been friends of Death, had played with him, had seen him repeatedly, watched his antics and indulged his whims. And now, there he was at the side of them, listening to what was said, ready to take a hand.

At those last words of Gracken it was Gracken himself who fired. He shot from his pendulous hand. In the palm of his hand—which was large enough for the purpose—he must have been holding a weapon concealed for some time past.

The shot had scarcely barked before Max also fired.

Then, in obedience to some reflex swifter than any modern training, they had gripped each other, swayed through the door. Inside the door for a dozen seconds it was a straining dance. They thumped against the door, and the door banged shut. There in the blue twilight of the deserted rooms Miss Bancroft had occupied they were two cumbrous, panting shadows—dark entities such as might have been conjured up by black magic from the Pit.

There followed two or three more shots. Followed this a swifter vortex of blood and breath.

Then Gracken swiftly collapsed—like something not entirely human. His own weapon had been flung from his hand. He sat there on the floor, propped up on one stiff arm looking up at Max. Even now his big face appeared calm, although dominated by a growing wonder.

"Comrade!" he panted. "Comrade!"

"I'm not your comrade—by the soul of God!"

Max was reeling slightly, but he still held his pistol in his hand. Still holding it, he dropped to his knee at Gracken's side so that their faces were close together.

"Look at me," droned Max between his teeth. "Do you still think I've worked all this time—for you?—for—Prussia?"

"You spoke German—like a—like a—"

"Your own curse returns on your head. You made me learn German. You put me in your schools. You beat me. You drilled me. You thought you were making a Prussian. But all the time I was—"

"Alsatian!"

"Alsace!—the child of France! Enslave her, will you? Lord-God—of heaven!—and Alsace! —and France! Me—I work for—Thou—and them!"

There was one more shot in the stifling shadows. There was a shadow that stumbled away and became articulate in prayer.

Mrs. Nichols, waiting on the quay with various other passengers for permission to board the leisurely *San Carlos*, felt an arm creep about her shoulders. It was an embrace so tender, so electric with affection, that for a moment or two she was almost persuaded that her old mind was deceiving her and that here in the Spanish city her granddaughter, Marjorie, had somehow appeared and found her.

Slowly she turned and looked up.

"Why, Ruth!"

"My dear friend," whispered Miss Bancroft; "my dear, motherly friend!"

"What's the matter, child?"

"Nothing," the girl replied. "I'm to go with you aboard the *San Carlos*. There's a boat waiting for us. We'd better go. There's danger here—danger all about us."

"And Max?"

"Perhaps he will join us later," said Miss Bancroft. "We're to wait for him until the second whistle blows."

At the place Max had indicated earlier in the evening they found the boat Max had provided for them. The boatman was old. It wasn't so surprising, perhaps, that he spoke a perfect French. Corunna had always been an important point of call for French liners bound for or returning from the tropics. A regular old gentleman the boatman was. He made the two ladies comfortable.

They all relapsed into silence.

Out across the tranquil waters of the harbour lay the *San Carlos*. Having already bellowed her first leviathan call she also had relapsed into the silence. Corunna glittered. Among the stars had appeared the moon—not quite so slender as when Mrs. Nichols had seen it a week ago in Northern France.

The moon could see—so she reflected—what was going on up there now—billowing smoke, raging flame, earth-thunder, the higher and finer drift of white soul-stuff. And a little later on this same moon would be silvering the pastures and church-steeples in far Vermont!

While her thoughts were thus engaged there came across the water from the direction in which the *San Carlos* lay a premonitory shaking of the air. The shaking became a vibration of huge sound.

The *San Carlos* was beginning its second blast.

Max, groping against the wall, made his way down the stone steps. He was almost at the bottom of them when some one entered the arched doorway from the street, sprang to greet him. It was the Spanish gipsy with his guitar still on his back. But the gipsy also spoke French.

"Gracken is dead," said Max; "but he's—he's—"

"Captain," the gipsy implored. "Quick! your arm around me. There's a doctor around the corner who's a friend of ours."

Max shook his head, but he accepted the other's aid.

"Help me to get to the boat," he commanded. "I learned it from something—Gracken had in

his pocket. The papers are going out—on the
San Carlos!"

They said more, but not much. Max's orders
were to be obeyed. A man of consequence he
was. The gipsy—call him that—knew that
both moments and breath were precious. Nor
could he have failed to see that neither of these
remained in great quantity to this youth who
had been his chief.

Around the end of the port they went, stick-
ing as much as possible to the shadows. But
their progress was slow. It was all Max could
do to keep his feet.

The boat was still half a mile away when
that tremulous voicing went up and out from
the finally active *San Carlos*. Max's strength
failed.

There on the smooth, cool cobblestones, the
double spy prepared himself to bid the world
good-by. He opened his shirt. From inside
of it he took something which he kissed and
then passed to the gipsy.

"Thou, Paul, run like the devil," he said,
"and give this to the girl whom you know.
Tell her—I'll see her—later!"

CHAPTER XXIII

BETWEEN TWO SHORES

RUTH BANCROFT was crying softly with Mrs. Nichols' arm about her as up from the launch they went to the steamer's lofty deck. For the girl had received that parting gift from the man she loved. She had recognised it—read the message of it—that emblem of the Legion of Honor! In these last weeks she had come to suspect. At last, owing to those events at the French frontier and in France itself, she had come to know. Yet no word had passed between them. That might have meant a violation of his oath, and this was war.

But that he was in the French service, while posing as a German spy—at instant peril to his life—that had come to be her secret as well as his, had come to be one more bond between them.

It made her feel infinitely base in comparison with him. Base she had been—base and unworthy, unworthy not only of him but of her own nationality. So she told herself.

And now, almost her last word to him had been a lie—a lie which her conscience had dictated, it is true, but one which nonetheless may have been the cause of his death. When he had asked her if she suspected where those papers might be, she had suspected. She had almost known. And yet she had answered in the negative.

By the irony of circumstance it so often happens that for duty done there is likewise remorse—almost as often as for meaner deeds.

Wasn't this a case in point?

For on the brief ribbon attached to the cross of honor which Max had worn there was a slight stain of darker red. Yes, he would see her again! See her again! That was the promise which many a man was giving to many a woman these days, but the meaning of it was no longer to be taken in an earthly sense.

The *San Carlos* eventually began to throb. Her propellers churned. Around the harbour rim the clustering twinkles of Corunna began to revolve in a stately march past. The breeze freshened—became slightly more salt, less tinged with the abiding aroma of oil and garlic, wine and sardines. Quite mysteriously, the lofty light at the port entrance drifted nearer, flashing more and more majestically. Only the moon and the stars were going along. The *San Carlos* was under way, outward-bound—bound for America.

Mrs. Nichols had a small, cheap cabin between decks. Ruth Bancroft had been allotted one of the large cabins on the promenade deck. In the excitement and confusion incident to sailing, however, there was no special occasion to notice this. The polite stewards were busy. The respective numbers of the state-rooms were given, and Mrs. Nichols departed in the wake of one steward, while Miss Bancroft followed another.

They had embraced each other. They were to meet each other again almost immediately. The long voyage lay ahead of them. And yet each woman, perhaps, just now was feeling as never before the need of solitude.

Not so very much larger than the state-room she had occupied while crossing the Lake of Constance was this other state-room allotted to Mrs. Nichols. But this, like that former one, was large enough. She could think in it. She could pray in it. In it she could rest and dream, and commune with all the spirits of the world. She could open the steel walls of it on vistas of Europe and America.

And wasn't it become a treasure-house?

She took the packet of letters from her
breast. She looked at it. Lo, it was become
as the Holy Grail! It was surrounded by a radiance. It was a symbol of Infinity on Earth.
Mere contact with it was blessedness.

"Verily," she whispered, "He hath not dealt
so with any nation!"

She sat there for a while longer. Again she
whispered:

"Into the hands of our President!"

From her own cabin Ruth Bancroft came out
upon the promenade deck. There by the rail she
stood watching the last light of Spain recede.
What lay back of her? What lay ahead? She
felt as if she herself had tasted of death. Back
there lay earth—or was it hell? Ahead lay
heaven. Between two shores she was in fact—
spiritually in fact—as much as any other soul
turned loose this night up there in Northern
France, or on the long Russian line, or in Pal-
estine, or out here on the ocean. Between two
shores—like the one man she had loved, and
who had kissed her good-by only a few hours
ago, and who had sent her word that he would
see her again.

Very remote indeed were her thoughts from
ordinary matters of this earth when she heard
a light tread back of her, heard a man clear his
throat, caught the aroma of a cigar.

She stood motionless.

There was a second or two of suspense, then
the intruder was moving on. Not until then did
Miss Bancroft venture a look in his direction.

"*Adios! Adios!*" came the hail as a dark
fishing-boat fled past.

The ship, with the invisible Spanish shore
dropping rapidly astern, was dipping into the
danger-zone. That flag, painted on her sides,
was now brightly illuminated. But the danger
from mine or submarine thus indicated was not
what quickened Miss Bancroft's pulse just then.
It was something familiar she had noted in the
presence in the man who had just passed.

In obedience to some sudden impulse, apparently, he had tossed his cigar overboard. He
himself had turned to the rail not so very far
from where Miss Bancroft stood.

She shuddered and waited. Yet she couldn't
be sure.

The long deck seemed to be deserted save
for herself and the man of the cigar. He had
turned and was looking at her through the
gloom. He strolled a little closer. He adopted

an air of carelessness, looking out to sea again;
but Miss Bancroft kept her eyes on him.

He had a rather prominent nose. Under his
longish, carefully brushed moustache his chin
did not appear particularly strong. He was
not very tall, nor very robust. His shoulders
were inclined to develop a pronounced stoop
whenever he allowed himself to sag, as he was
doing now. And yet, what was that hint about
him of all that she had fled from?—the military
absolutism?—the cunning?—the fierce and material cynicism?

The stranger made an odd pass with his hand.
Involuntarily, mechanically, before she could
check herself, she had returned the signal.

He drew close to her, stood there leaning on
the rail without looking at her. She could have
killed him. Herself she wished dead. But
through her fury, against him and against herself, there quavered some hint of hope. She
might serve, but not in the way this man
thought. His whisper somehow confirmed her
hope. It had come to her in German:

"Gracken is dead, but the work goes on."

"Dead?"

"Hadn't you heard?"

"No! I came out to the steamer early."

"Max killed him!"

Her heart thrilled. That was what Max had meant when he suggested that he might know where the papers were. He had believed Gracken to have them in his possession. Her silence was misinterpreted by the other. He was still lolling on the rail, had not looked at her.

"But Max also was killed. It was the last word that reached the boat. Fortunate it is that Gracken had his plans so well laid before the end came."

She was suffocating with the desire to ask what these plans were, but she merely remarked:

"Fortunate indeed!"

It was just as well for her that she had about exhausted her available stock of emotions, could appear calm when she heard what followed.

CHAPTER XXIV

A MIDNIGHT CALL

MRS. NICHOLS did have the papers. At last, the German Intelligence Department was certain of it. The knowledge had brought Gracken to Spain. It had caused Gracken to insure the sailing on the *San Carlos* of one of his best men. This was that man, booked on the cabin list as Amos R. Sutherland, of Philadelphia. Miss Bancroft herself was unsuspected—not only unsuspected, but credited with having arrived near the truth on her own account. Why else had she pretended such a friendship for the old American woman?

"I'll get the papers from her," Ruth Bancroft told the false Sutherland.

"You've been telling me that for the past three days," he snarled. It was true. For three days now the *San Carlos* had ploughed westward—far south, against a westerly breeze, soft and tropical. To the anxious passengers on the *San Carlos* it seemed as if the breeze was from America itself, and that America was near. "Three days," Sutherland repeated, "and we haven't a moment to lose. Who knows when a Yankee patrol will show up!"

"I'll get them," Miss Bancroft repeated; "but it takes caution. I have to watch my chance."

"Watch your chance! Bah! An old woman!"

They were standing on the boat-deck, with nothing but the sky and a few tireless gulls about them. Sutherland gave the girl a sly glance. There was an expression on her face he did not like. He was beginning to suspect that she wasn't as keen as she should be.

"Violence would merely make trouble," breathed Miss Bancroft.

"Is that so?" whispered Sutherland furiously. He made up his mind. "I'll show you. I'll get those papers myself—to-night!"

"To-night!"

"You heard me!" The man who called himself Sutherland kept his eye on the girl. He was trusting her now less and less. Coupled with this decreasing trust in her was a growing dependence on himself, together with an increasing fierceness, an access of tense strength. There was a good deal about the fellow to suggest a flabby and lethargic snake finally roused. "You heard me! To-night!"

"How! What will you do!"

"You'll get me the key of the old lady's stateroom. The state-room is Number Ninety-nine. I've been there often enough. But at night she locks the door. You'll get the key. You can do that much, can't you!"

"Yes!"

"And I'll do the rest. I'll show you—and her!"

Ruth Bancroft secured the key of stateroom Number Ninety-nine that afternoon. It wasn't a difficult feat. She and Mrs. Nichols were much together—while in the offing lolled and loitered and lurked that loose and lethargic snake which could so easily tighten up its coils and its wrath for hot, spasmodic action. Sutherland indeed! Another good American! Bound for Philadelphia, forsooth! And in the girl's changed heart was a deathly fear.

The fear was there when she turned the key over to the spy. Had he been a real snake, fanged and ruthless, her chill and shudder could not have been more intense. This man was a killer.

But her fear was gone—gone absolutely—

that evening when she seated herself at the dinner-table at Mrs. Nichols' side. On the other side of the table, a few seats further along, sat Sutherland—discreet and silently offensive but no longer terrible. Rather to be pitied he was— so complacently horrid; just like a snake!

"I have been up again to look at your state-room," said little Mrs. Nichols, looking slyly up at Ruth. "I'm afraid that I shall never be able to sleep in the midst of all that luxury."

Miss Bancroft was praying that Sutherland would not hear. He gave no sign.

"Just try it once—just for to-night," she whispered.

"But, dear, I can't deprive you of your quarters like this. La! It doesn't matter to me where I sleep. It will be different for you. You'll find it very hot and stuffy—"

"We've discussed all that," Ruth remarked softly, with smiling restraint. "Let me put some ice in your glass!"

Sutherland was a rapid eater. He never appeared to chew his food. His movements were leisurely. But the meal, whatever it was, disappeared smoothly and swiftly into his wide, weak, cruel mouth. Like that he finished his dinner now. He shifted himself into gliding action. He was gone.

Had he heard?

Ruth wondered. But as soon as he was gone she released her contained emotions in a flood of tenderness for the old lady at her side. It hadn't been easy for her to induce Mrs. Nichols to exchange state-rooms with her. But that was what she had done. The ship was still on the southern course. Mrs. Nichols had made some remark about the increasing heat. The remark had been the inspiration for which Ruth Bancroft had sought and prayed in the new crisis which Sutherland's impatience had thrust upon her.

With her arm about Mrs. Nichols, she tenderly guided the old lady to the promenade deck, along the promenade deck to the door of state-room AA, which was Miss Bancroft's own.

Mrs. Nichols could not deny that she was more feeble than she ought to be, that she had not been sleeping as well of late as she usually did. She could dream but couldn't sleep. That was the trouble. While the ship cradled league on league across the rollers it was always Pennsylvania Avenue, and the Capitol in Washington that was before her mental sight, and then the White House, and then the President.

Ruth Bancroft kissed her.

There for a moment Mrs. Nichols' meek, sa-

gacious eyes were looking into her own. One
would have said that the old lady suspected that
here also was the working of a divine plan.
This girl was greatly changed since that night
she wrangled with that man of the boarish eyes
in the Swiss train. Anyway this was what
Mrs. Nichols said:

"You're a pure and noble girl."

It was a blessing after a manner—a blessing
which Ruth Bancroft carried away with her a
little later as she went back alone along the
dark deck. Outside the smoking-room she lingered. Through a cleft in one of the curtains
she could look in. She saw Sutherland seated
alone, motionless, silent. He was not even
smoking. His cap shaded his eyes. In his
pocket she knew was the key to that small, ob-
scure state-room between decks.

He was waiting. He was implacable. When
the time came he would strike.

The murmuring silence of the sea and the
ship was softly reft by a peal of bells. Only
two of them—nine o'clock! There was still
plenty of time. The snake would not hurry.

She went aft. She stood there at the rail
looking back toward Spain. There Max had
died. Was he keeping pace with her? Would
she see him again? That had been his promise.

She thought of Mrs. Nichols. She quested into
the night for some answer to the old, old riddle
of the universe. Had Mrs. Nichols found that
answer? And if so, couldn't she also find it?

That part of the ship where she stood was
unlighted, but this merely gave an added lumi-
nosity to the ocean. She could see the phos-
phorescence foam and fade in the plunging
wake. She could follow the huge design of the
vast and lonely hills of water which appeared
and disappeared. There for a while she was
looking upon all this as one translated might
look upon the whole earth and the people there-
of—a creation of unrest, of dim light, and the
perpetual murmur and surge of a voice.

For the sea had a voice. It came to her as
vast and incomprehensible as the sea itself—
something restless and tortured and yet there
with a purpose.

Gradually, out of all this vastness there
evolved a personality. Once in her life had
she loved.

"Max!" she whispered.

The life she had led had not been conducive
to spiritual development. But she was conscious of that profound change of which she
was capable—even if she was not already transformed. Else, why should she thus send out

her soul in quest of one who could not hear?
Absurd she would have called such an action
on her part just a short time ago. Yet now
she repeated that whisper again:

"Max!"

There for a moment or two she was almost
certain that he could hear, that he did still live,
that there was a tenderness and a brightness in
her outlook such as she had never known before.

Then she heard—fine and strident through
the roaring of the waters—the rip and sputter
of the wireless telegraph. She sought to adapt
this physical miracle to her own mood and circumstances. What if she should receive a message out of space? Weren't others doing it?
Why not? Why not?

But it was with a heaviness of heart that she
finally turned and retraced her steps. She felt
herself weakening. Instead of the elation she
had hoped for she experienced nothing but a
numbing misery. In her life she had done many
things she wished she had not done. She
blamed herself, and at the same time she felt
a dull, unreasoning rebellion against the initial
Cause.

It was a mood that persisted all the while

she made her way through the unfamiliar com-
panionways of the lower deck, through suffocating corridors, over padded carpets and
brassy sills that threatened to trip her up, that
gave her traitorous excuses to hesitate and
change her mind. It persisted, even, when she
found the door of stateroom Number Ninety-
Nine, and entered there—stood there palpitating in the thick darkness—face to face at last
with the ultimate decision.

It was still not too late. She would go away
and remain away. The snakelike man who
called himself Sutherland would find the state-
room vacant. She could appeal to the officers.

But how about Mrs. Nichols? How about
those papers which the old lady had so won-
derfully brought thus far?

No; there was only one thing to do.

Room dark—nothing but darkness in her outlook now—she went about her dispositions.

Eight bells!—midnight!

She couldn't have told whether she had actually heard the familiar sound or not. Perhaps it was a knell in her brain instead.

She was lying in the berth Mrs. Nichols had
thus far occupied. That mood of darkness was
still upon her—a pall, funereal—darker than any

physical darkness. She had heard the brushing movement of something that crept closer and closer to the stateroom door.

She heard the delicate rasp of a key in the lock.

CHAPTER XXV

LET THERE BE LIGHT

RUTH BANCROFT did not move. She scarcely breathed. The key turned. The bolt slipped back. The door softly opened. The dark was suffused by a transparent dimness. Through this she saw perfectly the contour of the man she feared. Then he had entered. He had closed the door behind him. And it was dark again.

There followed for the girl an odd and thrilling experience. If her heart had been a black landscape and this was the dawn coming up. That would have described it.

No sound; no movement; muffled gloom; and there, almost touching her, the serpent disguised in the form of a man, poisonous and quick, ready to strike!—and yet that creep of light over the very soul of her! She dared to breathe.

Sutherland—he who went by that name—did not appear to breathe. As yet, since closing the door, he had not moved. He lurked there in the darkness, looking and listening, without nerves, without emotions, without heat, uncanny, unhuman, self-complacent, with neither patience nor impatience, sure of his kill.

But Ruth breathed, softly and regularly. The only thing abnormal about her seemed to be her heart. Her heart was throbbing. Not from fear, though. It throbbed because of that change that was coming over her mood—the flush and tenderness and revelation like that of the dawn she had witnessed that morning in Switzerland when she was with Mrs. Nichols going up to Zurich.

With every throb of her heart something of the darkness was leaving her. It was more than a dawn. It was a purification. Like the pink mountain-top that could already see the sun there emerged her conception of what Mrs. Nichols meant by love, and why love meant always sacrifice. It was Mrs. Nichols who inspired the thought, but the thought itself hovered about the young man Ruth Bancroft herself had loved.

There was a whisper in her brain: "We'll see each other again;" and this time she knew that it was so.

What followed was swift and violent. As a

matter of fact there could have been no long
lapse of time even up to now. The intruder
had merely locked the door as a matter of pre-
caution, had stood there to assure himself that
all was quiet, to draw from some hiding-place
the weapon he intended to use.

No one to vanquish but an old woman! He
must have felt safe. There was a click, a blinding rush of electric light.

Sutherland stood there with his left hand still
on the electric switch. In his right hand was
an oddly long revolver with a protuberance at
the end of it. In the first flash the girl had
recognised the weapon for what it was—a revolver with a silencer on it.

Ruth Bancroft's revolver had no silencer. It
was the same weapon she had taken from the
overcoat of that other spy. Max had conserved
it for her as they made their way across France,
and across the Spanish frontier and beyond. It
was almost as if Max had known. Even this
thought, nebulous and fine, like one more rose-
coloured cloud to her psychic dawn, came to the
girl now. High excitement is often ethereal.

"*Du!*" whirred Sutherland.

There was no mistaking that look in his de-
generate and fearful face. He had come to kill,

but kill at leisure. This was the snake that had been stepped upon.

At the same moment both fired.

There was only that single spurt of flame from Sutherland's weapon, a plugging, muffled hiss. But the girl had fired twice—then twice again as the spy toppled, sagged, sank with drooping chin and shoulders, glazing eyes.

He was dead before his knees were on the floor.

On the floor he knelt—propped up by the cramped space—in an attitude of utter dejection—such as might be that of one who prays—but prays too late, and knows that he prays too late. Slowly he sagged, lower and lower, until he sat—with his face to the carpet now, hands out, still in an abandonment of supplication.

Wide-eyed, but still somehow exalted, Ruth Bancroft had crept from her berth, stood crouched against the furthest wall. She was still standing there, her exaltation having become a racing joy, when there were sounds of inquiry and excitement in the companionway outside. She stood where she was, communing with herself, and her past and her future, and speaking no audible word, while an officer and a steward or two knocked on the door and demanded to know what had happened within.

The girl was still standing there when the door was finally opened. It required some effort, for the door opened in, and he who had been known as Sutherland was apparently trying to hold the door shut—for all his present, belated devotions—as if he were ashamed to be found where he was, doing that which he was doing, in the state that he was in. But the men outside pushed the door open nonetheless.

At first, Miss Bancroft was the only one they saw. They thought she was uninjured. They thought she was a somnambulist. So one of the stewards said.

"The young lady stood there," he said, "only half dressed, and with her hair down, and with that revolver in her hand. But it was the look of her, I tell you, that gave us the creeps. Her eyes were open. But she looked as if she were asleep. And she didn't look frightened. She smiled like a saint."

It wasn't long before they discovered the full extent of the tragedy though. Later on, they were to bury the dead man at sea. His papers revealed nothing. He carried an American passport. His name was given therein as Sutherland. That was all. There were none to mourn. The sea was accepting more than its usual quota of dead men these days; and was not this one among the least heroic?

He had probably learned that a girl had exchanged state-rooms—as a mere act of kindness for an elderly lady—with Mrs. Sylvia Nichols. Armed, he had entered that room and had been shot to death. That was all that was ever known, the only explanation given, save by two on board the *San Carlos*.

A sordid tragedy!

And yet, why did that nascent dawn in the spirit of Ruth Bancroft persist, wax and grow brighter still—even when she was fully aware of all that had happened, and that she herself had been wounded, and was in danger of death?

Another sort of physical darkness had crept about her. There for a while she was in an agony of pain. Pain and darkness became a confusion informed only by the lethal smell of chloroform. Out of this abyss she struggled faint and sick. But that bright light inside of her never wavered.

"You did it for me!"

That was Mrs. Nichols' voice. That was Mrs. Nichols' hand on her forehead.

Ruth Bancroft spoke—or thought that she spoke:

"You—were—God's messenger!"

CHAPTER XXVI

LIBERTY

D R. MacGOWAN was Scotch. He was
about fifty. The colour of him and the
texture—and somehow the sweetness too which
underlay his rough surface—was suggestive of
heather and tweed. It was strange to find such
a man as surgeon on a Spanish boat. But this
was wartime, when individuals were apt to be
in strange places all at the behest of an authority which considered not the individual will.
At any rate, the ship's doctor of the *San Carlos*
was this Scotch medical man, and it was he who
superintended the removal of Miss Ruth Bancroft from the state-room to the ship's small
but otherwise perfect hospital.

The hospital was well forward on the boat-
deck. There were no other patients in it. The
windows of it were larger than the usual ports.
It was bright and clean.

And there Dr. MacGowan did his work. He
kept telling the girl that he would try to have

her so well by the time America was sighted
that there would be no difficulty at all about
getting her into the port of destination.

"And will you?" asked Mrs. Nichols, softly
and apart.

The Scot met her eye. To some extent they
were of the same breed. He shook his head,
doubtfully.

New York was the port.

Sylvia Nichols looked forward to it those
long hours she sat in the hospital at the girl's
side. The *San Carlos* was steady. The weather
was fine. There was a swaying cadence to this
floating universe that may have awakened in
the souls of both of them memories of the
cradle of time—when peace was as yet un-
broken, before Eve mourned Abel, when the
Lord God still walked in the garden in the cool
of the day. They were silent. They talked.

"I loved Max," said the girl. "He is dead.
He was all I had. He said that he would see
me again. This is the only way. I—I intended
to die—die, like him, in doing something—
brave!"

That was all she would ever say about that
sacrifice she had planned to help Mrs. Nichols
on her way, but Mrs. Nichols understood. Nothing could have increased Mrs. Nichols' devotion

to this girl, but it is possible that the facts of the case lent an additional poignancy to what was transpiring in the aged woman's heart.

There came a day when Mrs. Nichols spoke up with a voice that seemed to be not her own.

"Ruth, Ruth," she said softly; "you're going to get well!"

The girl smiled.

"Perhaps!"

It was the apathy as much as the wound she had received that was killing her.

"Our patient will recover," said Mrs. Nichols a little later to the Scot. "I feel it in my heart she will."

Dr. MacGowan was noncommittal.

"Now, if you could make her believe it," he mused. "She's lost a deal of blood. But she's strong. She's clean. What's missing is the will to live. Perhaps, now, if we could stimulate the spirit of the lassie!"

Her work, that, to stimulate the lassie—so Mrs. Nichols told the wide, salt breeze. Did she not recall a certain period of her own life when she also lacked the will to live?—when the merest additional blow might have been excuse sufficient to give up the ghost? Ah, well she remembered it, and on her memory she drew.

America!

Day by day the distance shortened.

The talk was all of America now—America of the past, when there were Mound-Builders and confederated Indians, but a continent chiefly clean and empty, ready for the Puritans and the Huguenots, the Spanish and the Dutch, the Missionary Fathers of Canada and the Great Lakes; then the America of the Revolution; then the America of the Civil War; after that, the America of the Spanish War, when the only half-grown giant, having freed itself, fought its first foreign war that others might be free.

And now America was ready to fight again— once more in the cause of liberty.

Its destiny seemed simply clear and beautiful to Sylvia Nichols. That America should fight for others seemed to her the only natural thing. In fact, it couldn't be otherwise. This was the glory. America was beautiful, strong and young. Like Jeanne d'Arc, America had seen visions. America also would follow her visions, become an everlasting inspiration.

"I'm also—going to America—to be free," whispered Miss Bancroft.

She was.

Dr. MacGowan came and went. He did everything that a medical man could do, and added to this the higher science of his personality—a personality as clear as a bonny burn.

"But she'll dee," he confessed; "short of a miracle, she will."

Predestination was in his creed. He knew grief, but he knew not revolt. Only in the Scheme of Things was order and beauty and human hope. He was doing his best. He did hope, and yet—

Thus the *San Carlos* came safely across an ocean where stranger monsters lurked than any represented on the old Spanish maps. One night, out of the soft darkness, there flashed a distant star, low down on another invisible horizon; and that was America herself signalling to the homecomers that she was awake and waiting.

The ship went through quarantine at dawn. In the early morning light she crept up the channel toward the wonder-city.

Throughout all the latter part of the voyage, Sylvia Nichols had not once left Ruth Bancroft's side. She remained in the hospital. No more could she have left a babe of her own sinew and spirit, and that child sick, than she could have left this last child of all whom the colossal travail of Europe had entrusted to her keeping.

"Let me see," whispered the girl.

The Scotch surgeon was right. That bullet-wound she had received for Mrs. Nichols' sake was killing her. Perhaps the girl herself had no more delusions about this. Her strength was gone. Nothing but her beauty remained—and this was greater than ever—as beauty out of which has gone all weakness. But, as yet, no miracle.

Nonetheless the girl and Sylvia Nichols were glad.

There could be no doubt as to that. It was a sort of inexpressible gladness, so keen that it hurt.

For over the home-port there was a bluish haze. This haze was aquiver with filtered sunlight. The water was so calm and also brilliant that the ship seemed to be afloat in the atmosphere—the special atmosphere of some new star toward which the voyagers drew near from out of space.

A few white gulls circled about—intensely white in that special atmosphere.

Then the new world itself began to emerge—the peaks and minarets of a few lofty, unearthly buildings sketched in white sunlight—all this amid the brooding calm and silence.

"Look! Look!" whispered Sylvia Nichols.

She had raised Ruth Bancroft's blond head

on her arm. The girl did not speak, but she saw.

Out of the blue mist straight ahead had appeared something else. It might have been America herself, in person, gracious and hospitable, strong and sweet—the great figure of a woman with her light uplifted.

"Oh—oh—" breathed Ruth.

Dr. MacGowan came in. Into even his stolid face there had come some hint of a supreme excitement. Into his hand there had come a tremour.

"It's the miracle," he whispered, apart.

"I thought—I thought that if she saw—her country," Mrs. Nichols began.

" 'Tis not that," cried Dr. MacGowan; "but this!"

In his hand he held a message just received by wireless. He held it up. His voice broke:

"He lives!"

"Who?"

"The mon named—*Max!*"

Not then—but not long afterward—they gave that full message to Ruth Bancroft. Strong medicine it was—to be given in small doses, and yet each dose a potent infusion of new life, new hope:

Am safe in France—getting well—as will France—
and America—whatever the wounds—love follows
you—wherever you go—for we—are allies—forever!

"France and America wounded! Both getting well!"

It was Ruth Bancroft's whisper. There was
a symbolism in it. For, hadn't these two lov-
ers fought for freedom, as had their parent nations?

"Liberty!" breathed the girl again.

Her eyes were on the statue. Liberty returned her smile.

Ruth Bancroft to live. Max to live. Predestination was his creed, and Dr. MacGowan
now saw—as did Sylvia Nichols, in her wise old
heart—that not only would they live but find
happiness—as those soldiers will, in their several ways, who have fought for the liberty of
the world.

This much was agreed upon.

The wounded girl would receive the best of
care in a private hospital until she was strong
enough to travel. Then she was going to rejoin
Mrs. Nichols in the Vermont town, become a
daughter to her against that day when came
peace—and the Alsatian who had refused to
become anything but French, but might, pos-

sibly, for his wife's sake, some day become a good American.

There was a parting.

"And you're a fine, brave woman," said Dr. MacGowan, huskily, as he bade Sylvia Nichols good-by, perhaps forever. "Also, you're a better doctor than am I."

Doctor enough was he to see that there was a weakness and a heaviness of heart about Mrs. Nichols herself.

"For liberty—the liberty of the world!"

The words were whispering through all the corridors of Mrs. Nichols' heart and brain as she bade the doctor farewell in the vasty wharf. It was a whisper that must have been in the heart of Paul Revere when he made his famous ride, and of Mollie Pitcher when she fired the cannon, and of Key when he wrote his song.

"For liberty—men have died—and women, too; but I must not—shall not die!"

Almost at the end of her strength, and of her money too, was Mrs. Nichols as she emerged from the pier into West Street. She appeared even older and more shrunken than she had that night when she was leaving Germany. For here was a colossal activity, naked and primordial. Buildings were mountainous. There was a thunder of trucks and trains. Leviathan ships spewed and rumbled from their sea-caves. In and about and everywhere swarmed the incessant and innumerable crowds.

Was it possible, she asked herself, that she could be of any importance to all this?

She was having a momentary debate with herself. .

She was fiercely homesick now—fairly panting to get back to Vermont and find out what was transpiring there. No one had met her at the boat. She had received no word. Had a boy been born? Or was it a girl? Was Marjorie well? Or was Marjorie dead?

Her heart swelled up with a need for tears.

But she wouldn't give in.

All of these things, and all of these people, she saw about her—they were America. They were the promise of a world set free. They were doing in their way what Samuel P. Thomas—and then Ruth Bancroft—had done in theirs. And she herself *was* a part of it all. She also was important so long as she had some personal need or desire she could sacrifice.

"Not to Vermont," she settled the debate; "but on to Washington! That was my promise. Before all else I'll put these papers *into the hands of our President!*"

CHAPTER XXVII

HOME!

THERE was no mistaking the fact that Washington was once more expectant of the supreme adventure. War! The blood-pressure of the Capital was high. It was a pressure that came not only from the hundred millions in the United States. The hundreds of millions elsewhere—from Patagonia to Saghalin, from New Zealand to Manitoba—were likewise expectant. To old-timers it recalled the days preceding the Civil War. The younger generation knew that this was a civil war where states were supplanted by nations.

The Senators and the Congressmen came and went. The visitors poured in. The telegraph and the post were raging floods. The newspapers, with a fine disregard for the rising price of paper, spilled out their extra editions.

Would it be war?

Or would it be peace?

Would America make the splendid flight with

the rest of the eagles?—or sit, greedy and sordid, mumbling her food with her eyes on the ground?

She would make the flight. It couldn't be otherwise. She was an eagle—nested on a rock, high up, far-seeing, loving liberty, accustomed to a fellowship with heaven. And yet there was always that distressing doubt. There were so many who were trying to take the eagle in a net, clip her wings, fatten her!

Mrs. Nichols felt this atmosphere—or was it merely something engendered by an old memory?—from the moment that she saw the faint and distant panorama of Washington from the train. She felt it more than ever as she groped her way with a palpitating heart through the magnificence of a new railroad terminal. But most of all she felt it as she came out into that broad avenue which she had seen that other time more than fifty years ago.

It was morning. It was Spring.

To her finer perceptions it seemed that not only the round earth was dynamic with pent up forces ready to express themselves in leaf and flower, but that the universe itself was dynamic—with a spiritual force. And of the universe this was the opening flower!

She stood there looking in the direction of

the Capitol. To her it seemed as majestic as
the throne of God. Close by a large flag play-
fully shut off her view with a soft deluge of red
and white, then graciously withdrew to let her
look again.

Brilliant sunshine, a pure sky, a breeze from
across the Potomac perfumed with the smell of
Spring!

There was a surge of splendid choral harmony all about her. To serve! To be a soldier! To die that all this might live! How
gracious Thou art, O Lord, to have let me give
a husband and a son!

But her knees went weak. She had expected
to walk, because her funds were so low. Even
as it was, she didn't have enough left to pay
her fare to Vermont. And she wasn't quite
sure she knew the way to the President's house.
Washington was changed. There were so many
large buildings that had come into existence
since her previous visit.

The motors whirled past—taxicabs and li-
mousines. That other time—

It was as if she saw the self-same vehicle she
had taken then. It was coming near. It displayed no haste. That equipage wasn't designed for speed. It was an ancient victoria,
spindly-wheeled, drawn by a flea-bitten old

horse, skippered by a negro. The negro had white wool. His shoulders were bent. His wrinkled old face was graven into lines of dignity and kindness.

Did he recognise her?

He had halted his horse just in front of where Sylvia Nichols stood. He slowly saluted.

"Whar to, madam?"

Mrs. Nichols controlled herself and found her voice:

"To the White House!"

The black coachman drew up his bent shoulders somewhat. He lifted his old plug hat. Mrs. Nichols took her place on the worn cushions. The old horse arched his neck. Wasn't it just possible that he also had understood the name of their destination? Thus proudly they all went off together as if this were happening—befo' that other war.

There were soldiers on duty. The approaches to the White House were guarded. Even so, it was not an hour at which visitors usually arrive at that old palace—"at the other end of the Avenue." This being so, what was it that escorted Sylvia Nichols through the lines? Let the question remain unanswered. But it was, in fact, as if that title conferred by Ruth Bancroft—"God's Messenger!"—found an expression in a certain majesty, a certain pomp, a certain holiday, fluttering, band-music pageantry that dissipated opposition before opposition could oppose.

So it was right down the Avenue itself—something well-nigh inexpressible.

It was as if the negro and his chariot and she who rode therein were surrounded by some clattering, light-footed white-horse cavalry, guidons fluttering, sabres aglint, uniforms flashing above the silken haunches and tossing manes; while the school-children and their elders banked the sidewalks to sing and cheer; while the brass horns trumpeted and blared and rioted out their confusion of gay, triumphal music!

"Oh, see, God's Messenger is come!"

But more than all this intoxicating, present but unseen parade of the glitter and the glory and the power of the Republic, little old Mrs. Nichols, in her black alpaca, meek and wonderful, was conscious now as never before of the Presence. Just that! Silent, it kept her company—the great White Angel—something that encompassed her with a movement of mighty wings, with a sword of light, gentle and overwhelming.

Not for her, but for This, were the flags

afloat, and the regiments mobilised, and the people expectant as for a cosmic Jubilee!

At the entrance to the White House grounds the sentinels were on guard. Two civilians, as keen and compactly alert as bull-terriers, stepped out from some unsuspected lair. The old negro saluted with his whip. The sentinels lost for a moment their military bearing. Black soldiers they were—from one of the negro regiments—and negroes, so they say, often possess a second sight. But how about those white civilians? Did they also have the gift?

Through the guarded gateway went the visitor—without a challenge.

They were on the broad driveway that curves grandly around to the North Entrance of the mansion.

Mrs. Nichols was suddenly aware of the beating of her heart. She had seen an early-blooming crocus in the grass. The little flower recalled her home in Vermont. But it wasn't the thought that Vermont was still distant that made her heart beat like that. It was the thought that right here, and now, with the white columns of the great residence rising up in front of her, she herself was—home!

CHAPTER XXVIII

AS ONCE BEFORE

THE secretary to the President, not expecting visitors at this early hour, and himself so busy that each minute was well-nigh priceless, listened with a note of wonder to the announcement of the messenger that there was a lady out there who insisted on seeing the President.

"The President! That's impossible."

"Yes, sir."

The secretary thought of a dozen things. He was bitten by a premonition. These were prodigious times.

"What did you say her name was?"

"Mrs. Sylvia Nichols."

The secretary was unfamiliar with the name. Yet it was odd that the messenger, a veteran of the White House service, should hurry on of his own accord:

"She's all right, sir. All that she would tell me, though, was that she had to see the President personally—that she had just arrived from Europe—from Germany—"

The secretary let himself go for a moment or two in concentrated thought.

"I'll see her," he announced.

There was not an instant to lose. He stepped out swiftly into the great white and yellow vestibule. But it was a moment longer before he saw the visitor. She was still standing there near the glass doors leading from the porch— so little and old, so utterly tired, sad, broken, unarrayed, assailed by grief, homesickness, overwhelming modesty, that the secretary felt his heart give a little lurch.

Then she had stepped forward, with a sort of gentle and apologetic assurance, to meet him, and he was greeting her.

"The President is very occupied."

"He must be. I am so sorry to have to disturb him."

"May I ask—the nature of your business with him?"

"I have brought certain papers which I promised—promised a young man who is dead—to place in the President's hands. I know how busy he is—dear soul! I shan't detain him but a moment."

"Madam, I am the President's secretary."

Mrs. Nichols' face was illuminated by a beautiful and reminiscent smile. Hitherto she had continued to be somewhat overcome, perhaps, by the unexpected magnificence of the transformed vestibule—the white columns and the palms, the imposing spaciousness and solitude of it. But at the mention by the secretary of his identity it was apparent that Mrs. Nichols forgot something of this modern splendor.

"I was received by the President's secretary when I came here before," she announced happily. "It was right in this same room, only it was very crowded, with officers in uniform and statesmen and backwoodsmen—I remember that there was one dressed in buckskin; and there were a great many ladies, some of them very gorgeously dressed but a good many of them in mourning. And I was sure that the secretary would never find me. But he did. He was so polite and gentle, and brilliant and good, that—"

The secretary, about to speak, postponed his question.

"—I knew," Mrs. Nichols continued with subdued but rising enthusiasm, "he was destined to even greater things. They called him 'Major,' then; but later—when the whole world was honouring him, he was just 'Mister'—"

"Who?"

"Mr. Hay—John Hay!"

The secretary was comprehending how the White House guardian had been sufficiently impressed to let this caller break in upon him when so many things were shrieking to be done. The vestibule went shadowy—crowded with ghosts, so one would have said, of all the great men who had come and gone; and of one particularly, that predecessor of this present secretary whom the old lady had mentioned. From the old lady herself—a shrivelled figure in black, to the eyes of the flesh—there certainly emerged a spiritual presence, something greater and brighter, which shimmered and shone.

"Follow me," he said in a voice which was little more than a whisper. "I'll see—"

Perhaps much experience and a natural endowment had merely made the secretary something of a genius in the matter of character reading. But there was that something else besides—a something half remembered in the growing stress.

She and the secretary crossed the vestibule. They passed beyond the pillars and palms into a great corridor.

There for a moment or two Mrs. Nichols—so she recalled it afterward—was aware of some one who appeared at the farther end of this corridor but whom she neither clearly saw nor recognised just then. Still the impression was there as the secretary threw open a door to the left and asked her to go in and make herself at home.

"At home!"

There was a portrait of Lincoln on the wall— a great, full-length portrait. She tottered to a chair well out in front of this. She folded her hands in her lap and looked up at it.

"Mr. Lincoln!"

Here in this room she had come into his presence, had been presented to him here by that other kindly and comprehending secretary, Major Hay! And even this room had been crowded also as the vestibule and corridor had been. Yet strangely Mr. Lincoln had appeared to be standing here alone—all alone—just as he was now, there in the portrait.

She was seated there like that, rapt and meditative, when the door was softly opened. It was as if a spirit-whisper had reached her again: *"The President!"*

Who was it who came thus announced?

Mrs. Nichols was not quite so agile as she would have liked to be. Most of the night she had been in the cars. She hadn't slept. On her arrival in Washington she hadn't felt hungry, so she had gone without her breakfast. But now, for the first time, she was conscious of a slight distress.

The fact that she was here in the White House was itself a tremendous fact. Her interview with the secretary had increased the poignancy of it. So had this portrait of Lincoln.

There for a dizzy second or two it seemed impossible to her that fifty years had elapsed since that previous visit. This was still the time of the Civil War. The President was still "Father Abraham"—"Old Abe"—"Mr. Lincoln!"—with the brigadiers and the bearded statesmen, the office-seekers and the mourners swarming in. Her own David had just been killed. *Their* David had just been born.

Like a swimmer circling upward from deep waters her mind struggled toward the light and air, up through all those years that lay between, until she was in Germany again, until she was witnessing again the death of young Samuel P. Thomas.

It was as if she were telling the story of it all—in flashes of a communication defter than speech—not to the portrait of Lincoln but to Lincoln himself.

Then she had risen to her feet. She felt her

hand taken in a friendly grasp. A friendly voice was bidding her to remain seated. She was looking into a pair of friendly, thoughtful eyes. If she could only rid herself of that illusion of the other President who had once before so addressed her. But it was impossible.

"The other time that I was here—" she began, breathlessly.

"I didn't know—"

"He looked so haggard, and I knew that he was grieving still because of Willie's death. Willie was his favourite son—"

She was recognising now this man who stood in front of her—recognising him from his published photographs, no doubt; but, in her own heart, it seemed to Sylvia Nichols that she had always known him. Into his grave and thoughtful face there came a certain look which surely she had seen before.

"Oh, Mr. President," she said; "I've been so eager to help—now!—as I was eager then!"

CHAPTER XXIX

BIG NEWS

IT was with that quaver from her heart, summing up, so to speak, her entire life, that Mrs. Nichols, modestly and apologetically, yet with a certain devoted pride, brought from her breast for the last time the packet of papers she had so long carried there. But her emotions now were by way of getting the better of her. She tried to explain. She could only pass them over in silence.

It was her soul that spoke. Her soul cried out:

"Into his hands! Into the hands of our President! O Lord, Thy mission is fulfilled!"

Could the President have heard?

He had taken the packet. Gravely he considered it. His eyes dwelt on the flowered, old-fashioned ribbon that held the three envelopes together. He glanced at Mrs. Nichols. He must have gathered from her expression that it was not in her power to speak again just

·231

then. From the neighbouring wall, yet as a living witness, that other President looked on—gaunt and patient and luminous.

Now Lincoln's successor was confronted by such staggering vistas as Lincoln himself had known. Yet as Lincoln might have done he likewise bent his attention to this present thing.

He slipped the ribbon from its place. He studied the uppermost envelope—without haste—with kindly interest—with a studious concentration.

"From Lieutenant Nichols—dated 1863!"

"My husband," whispered Mrs. Nichols.

She was doing her best to explain, to command her breath to speech, and those two words were all that came. The President had turned with a subtle access of earnestness to the second envelope.

"From Lieutenant Nichols—and this one dated 1898!"

"My son!"

Mrs. Nichols was commanding herself to be strong—strong! She would have to explain. She would have to say that it was not the envelopes which mattered now. The President with no lessening of his courtliness, with no impatience, had turned to the third envelope. Then Mrs. Nichols, summoning all her strength, to hold back her tears and force out the necessary words, looked from the envelopes to the President's face.

"Open them!" she gasped.

The President as gently as ever opened the envelope which then happened to be on top. From it he drew out one of those tightly folded sheets that Mrs. Nichols had placed there at such cost while crossing the Lake of Constance. This sheet he unfolded. He looked at it curiously. There was a flash of incredulous amazement, then joy.

"My dear Mrs. Nichols," he exclaimed.

He took her hand. He helped her back into her chair.

"You don't know—what—what a service—you've rendered our Country," he was saying.

But Mrs. Nichols did know. There was that in the President's action and the President's voice that was carrying her back—back to that time, half a century ago, when Mr. Lincoln's voice had sounded like that when he spoke to her, using much those same words. Oddly enough it recalled her young widowhood.

She wept.

Later—very much later, it seemed to Mrs. Nichols—she was telling the President the whole story of how the papers had come into her possession, and of how she had brought them out of Germany, and across Switzerland, across France, through Spain, and over the ocean, and so on to Washington.

Also, although that had not been her intention, she must have told much concerning the three envelopes in which she had replaced the documents of a lesser by those of a greater love. She was a little confused at the attention she was receiving. But of this she was certain. She had such a sympathetic listener that this was no longer merely a great official to whom she spoke. It was a personal friend.

To one with ears better attuned to the machinery of state it might have been perceptible— that hum and whir of an almost delirious excitement.

"They've come! They've come! The papers are here!"

It was an excitement which filled the White House itself, which spread like a wind through the rooms and corridors to the out-lying Office Building—where secretaries laboured with a new intensity, where newspaper correspondents crowded the singing wires with bulletins about some great story soon to be released. It was an excitement which spread from department building to department building, on up to the great domed Capitol, where Congressmen and Senators suddenly caught the fervour and solemnity of it—this thing as yet undefined, but adventurous and grand.

Against all the cunning and might of an Empire a messenger had arrived in Washington with certain papers which the messenger had placed in the hands of the President.

And now it would be war—war for the freedom of all the peoples of the earth!

But Mrs. Nichols was merely the guest of this courtly gentleman, her friend. She was exceedingly anxious lest she bother him. She had merely wanted to give him the papers and then go right away again. But he insisted that she breakfast with him. She tried to refuse. He amiably commanded.

It was more than she deserved, however, when he repeated, gently and persistently, how deeply was the nation in her debt. She sought to change the subject. She spoke about her granddaughter, Marjorie.

"And I've been hoping so," she added softly, "that it will be a boy!—that he might grow up to be a soldier—to live, and to die if the Lord so wills, as his great grandfather and his grandfather did—for his Country! When the other war broke out—and I was nothing but a girl—

I used to wish that I was a man so that I might die like that. But I've learned since that girls —and wives and mothers—and grandmothers," she added with a brilliant smile, "can do their share."

There was a telephone on a table in a corner of the room. The President walked over to this meditatively.

"And you've had no word from your granddaughter?"

"She didn't know when to expect me. I was so concerned with what I had to do—"

"You've done it, magnificently!"

"—that I did not write—as I should have done."

The President picked up the telephone, spoke into it softly.

"P r e s i d e n t speaking!—Long-distance, please!—get me a clear line to Bennington, Vermont!—What was the local number?—Three six-seven!"

Mrs. Nichols listened breathlessly. But there was a hiatus in what she heard. It was while her own spirit was in flight to Bennington, in far Vermont, where events of such consequence must have come to pass. Again she heard the President speak:

"The mother is well, you say—and the child?

What's that?—They have called him—David!"

"Oh," cried Mrs. Nichols, in a burst of longing and relief, "a boy!—a boy to live and fight and labour for his Country's good!"

She had started to rise from her chair. She was overcome by a seizure of weakness. She was penniless. The last money she had in her purse she had given to the old negro coachman who had driven her on this last splendid stage of her mission.

But the President himself had bade her remain seated. He was speaking into the telephone again. He had asked for some local call. He smiled at her while he waited. He didn't have to wait long.

"This is the President speaking. How long before I can get a special train straight through to—Bennington, Vermont? No, not for myself—but the usual car—for a guest of the nation!"

The President himself escorted Mrs. Sylvia Nichols to the steps of the White House porch, when the time came for her to leave. There was a limousine waiting there to receive her instead of the ancient victoria that had brought her. There were two pleasant Secret Service men on duty there to act as her honorary escort from Washington to Vermont—to her home!

She paused there on the porch with the President at her side. She looked up at him.

"I'll write to the mother of that other boy—Mrs. Thomas, of Wooster, Ohio," she said sweetly, "and tell her—may I?—how highly he was considered by our President."

"Tell her," the President responded soberly, "as I myself shall do, that the nation intends to forget—neither him—nor you!"

He took her hand in his. Into his face came the look of a man whose vision is not altogether of the physical eyes. It was evident that there was much that he could, and would, have said. He had become the Commander-in-Chief again. As such he assisted her with veneration into the waiting motor-car.

He lingered there a moment longer.

"For with such as you," he added, "our Country shall become greater still—and live—forever!"

CHAPTER XXX

THE OLD WASHINGTON!

SOMETHING great had happened, like the advent of Spring in the world. Mrs. Nichols was aware of it as the luxurious and silent motor-car drifted outward from the White House grounds. The flags were brighter still. Brighter was the green of the earth and the blue of the sky. There was a tranquillity, but it was the tranquillity of a majestic power at work. That ebullition of joyousness—unseen but in evidence—on her faring to the White House was now replaced by a solemnity and grandeur.

Perhaps it was only a silence evolved from her own spirit—the sort of silence in which one hears again recently spoken words and reviews again places and figures recently seen. But gradually and insistently this silence all her own was penetrated by a cadence.

This cadence at first penetrated to her consciousness and there awoke an abiding mem-

ory. It was a distant booming, like that of big
guns, heard through the night, twenty or
twenty-five miles away. Eyes shut, she was on
the shores of the Lake of Constance again.
Eyes still shut she was in Northern France.
It was a vision of war.

But the booming was almost instantly over-
laid by other sounds more stirring still.

That was the booming of a bass-drum she had
heard. The other sounds were organized into
the harmony of martial music. Mrs. Nichols
with a palpitation at her heart opened her eyes
and leaned forward. This was Washington. It
was the old Washington, the one she had remembered and loved. The motor-car was sweep-
ing forward while the music swelled louder and
louder.

"Wait! Wait!" she cried, tremulously.

One of the Secret Service men heard her, or
anyway divined her wish. The motor purred
to a standstill.

Out from an adjacent street came the band
with a blare of heart-lifting music and a waving
flag. There were men on horses. There was a
regiment on foot. The crowds surged up.

It was a memorable day in Washington.

It was the day with the first sure augury of
conflict and victory. Just whence this augury

came none could tell. But this was the day that
there swept over Washington—and the rest of
the Country, perhaps—that presage of a new
era for America and the world. Men remember, and will continue to remember for many
years, their elation, their first glimpse of that
new dawn over cosmos.

The car moved on.

To that music of a kind to set the blood of
men on fire Mrs. Nichols bowed her head in
silent prayer.

THE END

PR...
&...
NEW V...
SOCIETY...

Trieste Publishing has a massive catalogue of classic book titles. Our aim is to provide readers with the highest quality reproductions of fiction and non-fiction literature that has stood the test of time. The many thousands of books in our collection have been sourced from libraries and private collections around the world.

The titles that Trieste Publishing has chosen to be part of the collection have been scanned to simulate the original. Our readers see the books the same way that their first readers did decades or a hundred or more years ago. Books from that period are often spoiled by imperfections that did not exist in the original. Imperfections could be in the form of blurred text, photographs, or missing pages. It is highly unlikely that this would occur with one of our books. Our extensive quality control ensures that the readers of Trieste Publishing's books will be delighted with their purchase. Our staff has thoroughly reviewed every page of all the books in the collection, repairing, or if necessary, rejecting titles that are not of the highest quality. This process ensures that the reader of one of Trieste Publishing's titles receives a volume that faithfully reproduces the original, and to the maximum degree possible, gives them the experience of owning the original work.

We pride ourselves on not only creating a pathway to an extensive reservoir of books of the finest quality, but also providing value to every one of our readers. Generally, Trieste books are purchased singly - on demand, however they may also be purchased in bulk. Readers interested in bulk purchases are invited to contact us directly to enquire about our tailored bulk rates. Email: customerservice@triestepublishing.com

You May Also Like

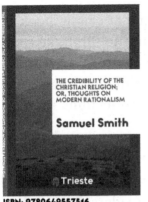

ISBN: 9780649557516
Paperback: 204 pages
Dimensions: 5.83 x 0.43 x 8.27 inches
Language: eng

The Credibility of the Christian Religion; Or, Thoughts on Modern Rationalism

Samuel Smith

ISBN: 9780649724185
Paperback: 130 pages
Dimensions: 6.14 x 0.28 x 9.21 inches
Language: eng

Report of the Second Annual Meeting of the Maryland State Bar Association, Held at Ocean City, Maryland, July 28-29, 1897

Conway W. Sams

www.triestepublishing.com

You May Also Like

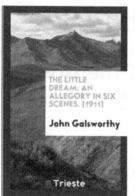

The Little Dream: An Allegory in Six Scenes. [1911]

John Galsworthy

ISBN: 9780649637270
Paperback: 50 pages
Dimensions: 6.14 x 0.10 x 9.21 inches
Language: eng

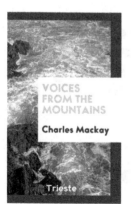

Voices from the Mountains

Charles Mackay

ISBN: 9780649730360
Paperback: 140 pages
Dimensions: 5.25 x 0.30 x 8.0 inches
Language: eng

www.triestepublishing.com

You May Also Like

ISBN: 9780649420544
Paperback: 108 pages
Dimensions: 6.14 x 0.22 x 9.21 inches
Language: eng

1807-1907 The One Hundredth Anniversary of the incorporation of the Town of Arlington Massachusetts

Various

ISBN: 9780649194292
Paperback: 44 pages
Dimensions: 6.14 x 0.09 x 9.21 inches
Language: eng

Biennial report of the Board of State Harbor Commissioners, for the two fiscal years commencing July 1, 1890, and ending June 30, 1892

Various

You May Also Like

Biennial report of the Board of State Harbor Commissioners for the two fisca years. Commeneing July 1, 1884, and Ending June 30, 1886

Various

ISBN: 9780649199693
Paperback: 48 pages
Dimensions: 6.14 x 0.10 x 9.21 inches
Language: eng

Biennial report of the Board of state commissioners, for the two fiscal years, commencing July 1, 1890, and ending June 30, 1892

Various

ISBN: 9780649196395
Paperback: 44 pages
Dimensions: 6.14 x 0.09 x 9.21 inches
Language: eng

Find more of our titles on our website. We have a selection of thousands of titles that will interest you. Please visit

www.triestepublishing.com

Lightning Source UK Ltd.
Milton Keynes UK
UKOW01f1510231017
311488UK00008B/2461/P